"**I need you to go to my sister's wedding with me…as my lover.**" Having broached the subject, Rourke quickly regained his composure.

"What?" she gasped out, sure she must have misheard somehow.

"I want you to attend the wedding with me."

She had that part—it was the other she took exception to. "As your lover?"

Rourke hastily held up a hand to forestall the protests he knew were hovering on her lips. "I didn't mean that the way it sounded. I need you to *pretend* to be my lover…."

It used to be just a nine-to-five job....
Until she realized she was

Now it's an after-hours affair!

Getting to know him in the boardroom...
and the bedroom!

Coming soon:
The Parisian Playboy
by
Helen Brooks

Harlequin Presents #2352
On sale in October

Amanda Browning

HIS AFTER-HOURS MISTRESS

In Love With Her Boss

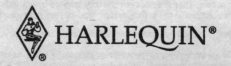

HARLEQUIN®

TORONTO • NEW YORK • LONDON
AMSTERDAM • PARIS • SYDNEY • HAMBURG
STOCKHOLM • ATHENS • TOKYO • MILAN • MADRID
PRAGUE • WARSAW • BUDAPEST • AUCKLAND

ISBN 0-373-12335-3

HIS AFTER-HOURS MISTRESS

First North American Publication 2003.

This edition published by arrangement with Harlequin Books S.A.

® and TM are trademarks of the publisher. Trademarks indicated with ® are registered in the United States Patent and Trademark Office, the Canadian Trade Marks Office and in other countries.

Visit us at www.eHarlequin.com

Printed in U.S.A.

CHAPTER ONE

GINNY HARTE jumped at the sudden sound of a crash from the office next door, and glanced round to frown at the closed door which linked the two offices. As far as she was aware, her fellow director of the family-owned chain of hotels, Roarke Adams, was still at lunch. Her fingers paused over the keypad of her PC as she waited for another noise. There followed the distinct sound of something large, probably the wastepaper basket, hitting a wall. An unholy grin slowly spread across her face. All had not gone well, it seemed. What a shame. Couldn't have happened to a nicer guy, she thought, with a wry grimace.

Pushing back her chair, she rose gracefully to her feet, walked round the desk and headed for the closed door and the momentarily silent room. She was tall, even without her three-inch heels. Slim yet curvaceous, she had flashing green eyes, and the tempestuous nature her thick swathe of red hair indicated. Experience, however, had taught her to keep it in check and now, at the age of twenty-six, she presented a cool, calm demeanour to the outside world.

She had worked alongside Roarke Adams for a little over a year now, ever since his grandfather, the owner of the hotels, had hired her to co-ordinate the modernisation and decorating of the various properties. All other aspects of the business fell into Roarke's court, but when he bought a new property it was up to her to decide what was needed to bring it into line with the other hotels. When he did his regular tours of the hotels she went with him to oversee any planned redecoration, and they had a surprisingly good working relationship. Which was nothing short of amazing considering the fact that they didn't actually like each other.

It had taken under a month for them to sum each other up and decide the other was wanting. Battle lines had therefore been drawn and their verbal exchanges had become a source of much interest and amusement to the staff. Skirmishes occurred on a daily basis unless one or other of them was out of the office. Roarke never missed an opportunity to get in a dig at her and, as she had never been one to refuse a fight, she gave as good as she got.

She knew he thought she had ice-water in her veins instead of blood. He didn't believe she had an ounce of passion in her whole body, and wouldn't know what to do with a real man. He viewed Daniel, her boyfriend, with open mockery because he was everything Roarke was not. Loyal, steadfast, undemanding. OK, so it wasn't a passionate relationship, but Ginny had trodden that path once, allowing her passions to rule her head, and it had led to disaster. It wasn't a road she intended to travel again. Daniel was what she wanted now, and she was pretty sure he was going to propose soon. When he did, she had every intention of accepting him.

If her lifestyle was a joke to her co-director, his was only worthy of her scorn. Roarke, in her opinion, was little more than an unprincipled womaniser. Women went in and out of his life in a more or less constant stream. Like a modern-day Casanova. Any woman who came within range was fair game to him, and even the strongest of them turned to jelly when he looked at them with his glittering eyes and disarming smile. It wouldn't surprise her in the least if he didn't carve a notch on his bedpost for every woman he seduced.

Though she didn't care for his love-them-and-leave-them lifestyle, she knew he was generous and knew how to treat a woman well, whilst his interest remained. And, to be fair, he never approached married women, or those who were otherwise spoken for. Roarke had a code of sorts. He only played the game with those women who knew the rules, and he never became involved with the women who worked for him. His life had two distinct areas, and the one only spilled into the other when she had to console the latest cast-off. A job she did not enjoy.

She had made her disapproval clear but, rather than taking offence, Roarke had been amused by it. He had mockingly informed her he wasn't going to be reprimanded by a strait-laced harridan. So it had begun, and that was the state of affairs between them now as she reached the connecting door. A wise woman might have drawn back, but Ginny recognised an opportunity when it presented itself. There was no way she could work on without knowing what had happened, so she reached for the door handle.

Pushing the door open, she had to duck hastily as an object hurtled in her direction. Straightening up, she stared down at the pencils which littered the floor around her like so much strange confetti, then back at the man who now stood immobile by the desk.

Honesty compelled Ginny to admit Roarke was, without doubt, the best-looking man she had ever seen. At thirty-two he was in his prime. Tall and leanly muscular, he had thick black hair, roguishly laughing grey eyes, and a mouth that could quirk into a smile to take the breath away. Right this minute, though, he wasn't smiling. On the contrary, his expression most closely approximated thunderous. It caused her lips to twitch.

'Nice lunch?' she enquired jauntily, and caught his fingers flexing as if he wished they were around something—like her neck.

His fine nostrils flared as he took a steadying breath. 'No, I have not had a nice lunch. In fact, I've just had the worst few hours of my life!'

'Don't tell me some little air-head actually had the sense to say no to you,' she drawled with heavy irony, and in a lightning mood swing he grinned at her.

'I don't date air-heads, sweetheart. I much prefer intelligent women; you know that,' Roarke drawled back, watching through glittering eyes as she squatted down and began to collect up the pencils. The process caused her skirt to ride up her thighs. 'Nice legs,' he murmured approvingly, then as she shot a narrow-eyed glare his way he changed tack. 'Did I hit you?' he asked with less than genuine concern, and Ginny snorted as she retrieved the holder and stood up again.

'No, but I might just hit you if you don't keep your eyes to yourself,' she warned as she set the holder on the nearest bookcase and folded her arms.

'It's your own fault for being so easy on the eye. A man just can't help himself,' he told her ironically.

He was flirting with her, a tactic he had used from time to time when he wanted to irritate her more than usual. She ignored it—as usual. 'Well, a man had better try,' she added firmly.

Roarke slipped his hands into the trouser pockets of his fashionable Italian designer suit, and rocked back on his heels. 'You're a hard woman. Does anything get through to you? Do you feel passion? Do you even know what it is? What about Daniel? How does that relationship work? Is he even allowed to kiss you, or does he go home each evening aching with frustration, whilst you sleep soundly in your virginal bed?'

Ginny kept her cool and raised her eyebrows at him mockingly. 'You don't really expect me to answer that, just because you're in a foul mood?'

'No, I expected you to up and slap my face. Why didn't you?'

She gave him an old-fashioned look. 'Probably because it was what you wanted,' she responded dryly and he laughed.

'You're learning, sweetheart. There's hope for you yet,' he taunted as he sauntered over to the window and looked out at the city below them.

'I'm not your sweetheart, Roarke. It isn't a situation I would ever aspire to occupy,' Ginny countered, though she didn't expect it to have any more effect than her previous attempts to have him stop calling her by the affectionate term.

He glanced over his shoulder at her. 'A man could get frostbite trying to warm you up. Daniel has all my sympathy.'

Ginny silently ground her teeth at his insolence. 'Fortunately, Daniel doesn't need it,' she said, which caused him to smile.

'No, he's pretty much a cold fish himself.'

She looked at him steadily. 'I don't find him in the least bit cold. There's a lot to the old adage that you shouldn't judge a book by its cover.'

'Which could equally apply to me, sweetheart,' Roarke pointed out, but Ginny immediately shook her head.

'Oh, no, you're an open book, Roarke. Everyone knows the plot where you're concerned. The wise ones put you back on the shelf,' she retorted mockingly, whereupon his eyes gleamed with mischief.

'Maybe, but the ones who don't have a much better time.'

Ginny shook her head sadly. 'You're incorrigible, and I have more important things to do with my time than waste it bandying words with you,' she told him bluntly, and made to leave, but Roarke held up a hand to forestall her.

'That can wait. Shut the door and sit down. I need to talk to you,' he commanded. His words were without a trace of his earlier mockery, and yet carried an edge of unease. Sensing something intriguing in the air, Ginny dutifully closed the door.

'I thought you didn't consider me qualified to be an agony aunt,' she remarked as she stepped over various objects which had borne the brunt of his temper.

'One of these days you're going to cut yourself on that tongue of yours!' Roarke warned her. 'Doesn't anything blunt it?'

'If you're after sympathy, you've come to the wrong woman,' she told him matter-of-factly. 'Just because you didn't get your own way for once, there's no need to destroy the place. So you met a woman with a brain cell or two. It was bound to happen some time.'

Roarke tutted reprovingly. 'You know something, Ginny? You're fixated with my love life. Who said this has anything to do with a woman?'

Now that did surprise her. Roarke was like a magnet for women. He didn't look dressed without one on his arm. That didn't mean to say he didn't work hard at the business. It wouldn't be among the top in its line if he didn't. But he played hard, too. She had listened to his tales of woe before, and a woman generally entered the picture at some point. But apparently not this time, if he was to be believed.

'It doesn't?' she queried, brows rising. If she had done injustice, then she was prepared to apologise, however much it went against the grain. She was about to open her mouth to do just that when his eyes fell away from hers and he rubbed an irritated hand around his neck.

'Actually, it is about a woman, but not the way you imagine,' he admitted reluctantly.

Intrigued by the palpable signs of his discomfort, Ginny slipped into the nearest chair and crossed her legs, decorously smoothing down the skirt of her violet-coloured suit. She had discarded the jacket earlier, and wore a simple cream silk sleeveless blouse for comfort in the oppressive summer heat.

'What do you imagine I'm imagining?' she challenged, her eyes following him as he walked to his leather chair and sank into it with a heavy sigh.

'The worst. You usually do,' Roarke shot back dryly, and Ginny laughed softly.

She spread her hands deprecatingly. 'Well, you've only yourself to blame for that. You've never had to console one of your exes. The tales I've heard make me shudder to think of them.' She gave a delicate shudder by way of example.

'Don't believe everything you hear. It isn't my fault if they got their hopes up. I never promised them for ever,' Roarke pointed out in his own defence.

'That's what I told them. He isn't a one-woman kind of man. You'd be better off cutting your losses and looking around for someone with more staying power,' Ginny agreed.

His brows rose at that, and then he laughed. 'You're referring, I take it, to that part of my life which I, clearly mistakenly, consider private. Hasn't anyone ever told you you aren't supposed to interfere in your employer's love life?'

'Your love life ceases to be private when you live it so

publicly. Why, scarcely a day goes by when you aren't photographed with one woman or another hanging on your arm! Your little black book must be bursting at the seams by now,' she protested scornfully.

Roarke steepled his fingers and looked at her over them. 'If I had one, which I don't.'

'No little black book? I don't believe it. Your sort of man always has one!'

'And just what sort of man is that?'

Ginny waved a hand airily. 'The sort who changes his woman as often as he changes his clothes.'

He tapped his thumbs together broodingly. 'I suppose a denial is out of the question?'

She shook her head. 'Hard to accept when I've seen the results of your handiwork.'

Roarke rubbed a finger down the bridge of his nose, then glanced at her sardonically. 'You disapprove of everything about me, don't you?'

'Not everything, just your treatment of women.'

'You make me sound like some sort of playboy.'

'Your affairs are well catalogued in print,' she reminded him.

He clucked his tongue at her. 'The women you see me photographed with are, for the most part, old friends. I'm often invited to events where I require a partner, and I'd rather take a woman I know than find myself seated next to a stranger. We spend an enjoyable evening together, and then I take her home. End of story.'

Ginny looked sceptical. 'You can't mean to tell me all your dates end so tamely,' she scoffed, and he grinned wolfishly.

'Not at all, but that's my business, not yours.'

She couldn't argue with him there. She was walking a fine line as it was. However, there was one thing she was curious about. 'Haven't you ever considered finding one woman and sticking to her? Haven't you ever been in love?'

That brought a mocking laugh from him. 'No, and I don't ever expect to be. In my experience, happy ever after is just a fairy tale, sweetheart,' he pronounced and she blinked, genuinely surprised.

'You don't believe in love?'

'What most people fall into is lust, though they prefer to give it the name love because it sounds better.' Seeing her frown, Roarke leant forward across the desk. 'I respect women for who and what they are. I enjoy them, but I don't make promises I can't keep, and I refuse to dress up the relationship as anything more than what it is.'

Ginny supposed she had to think well of him for that, but it was strange to her to hear him speak that way about love. Despite her own experiences, she still believed in love. She had just made the wrong choice, that was all. This time she wasn't about to let herself be blinded by passion into thinking love existed. Daniel was everything she wanted in a man, and she was sure that her liking for him would grow into love in the fullness of time.

'Don't you intend to get married and have children?' she couldn't help but ask curiously.

Sitting back again, Roarke shrugged. 'Sure, one day, but love will have nothing to do with it.'

'Your wife might disagree.'

'The woman I marry will know that she has my respect and loyalty. If and when I make a vow, I'll never break it. I only intend to get married once.'

'Sounds to me like you've had a nasty experience. What caused you to get so disenchanted with marriage?'

'Over-familiarity. My father has been married four times and my mother is currently on her third husband.

Both swore it was love each time, but as soon as the passion faded, they headed for the divorce courts. I have brothers and sisters dotted around the globe from their various forays into the wedded state.'

Not exactly good role models, she agreed. 'It doesn't have to be that way for you.'

He shrugged. 'It isn't going to be. I intend to honour my vows—when I make them.'

'I'm pleased to hear it, but have you heard the one about leopards not changing their spots?' she gibed.

Roarke smiled. 'There's always an exception to the rule, sweetheart.'

'True, but I haven't seen any flying pigs recently,' Ginny mocked.

He gave her a long look for that, to which she smiled sweetly and he grunted, 'I should have fired you months ago. Lord knows why I didn't.'

'Because it isn't in your power to do so. Your grand-father hired me, and only he can fire me,' she told him confidently, only to see him give a crocodile smile.

Tugging at the knot of his tie, he pulled it free and loosened the buttons of his shirt. 'On the contrary. I could fire you at a moment's notice. However, you're damn good at your job. You've a good eye for colour and style, and we've heard nothing but acclaim for what you've done so far.'

His praise gave her a warm glow inside, though she didn't let him know it. 'Would this be a good time to ask for a rise?' she asked, tongue-in-cheek, and he grinned appreciatively.

'You'd probably get it, too. A good worker is worthy of her hire.'

Ginny wasn't greedy. She had had a rise only a short while ago. The company rewarded its workers for their efforts without prompting, and she had received her share. That was enough for her. 'Don't worry, I have no intention of taking you up on that. So, what did the poor wastebasket do to incur your wrath?'

Reminded of what had happened earlier, Roarke let his expression become rueful. 'It grinned at me.'

Vastly amused, Ginny smiled. 'Grinned at you?'

'Knowingly,' Roarke confirmed.

'Ah,' she nodded wisely, knowing the feeling. 'Lunch was not a success.'

His laugh was scornful. 'To put it mildly. Which is why I need your help.'

Her mind was rioting with questions. Ginny reined them in. 'Things must be bad if you need my help.'

'You have no idea!'

Ginny waited for more, but when none came she frowned. 'Are you going to tell me, or is it a game of twenty questions?'

Roarke took a deep breath and swung his chair round so that he was facing her. 'My sister's getting married at the weekend.'

Whilst interesting, it was not quite what she was expecting. 'I'm sure I'm pleased for her, but what's that got to do with me?'

His eyes flashed sparks at her interruption. 'I was coming to that. I've been invited.'

It occurred to Ginny that he was uneasy about asking her for whatever it was, and that was quite unlike the usual confident Roarke Adams. Bemused, she nodded. 'OK, that was to be expected, but I still don't see what that has to do with me.'

There followed a momentary hesitation, then he took the bull by the horns. 'I need you to go with me...as my lover.'

That took the wind out of her sails like nothing else. 'What?' she gasped out, sure she must have misheard somehow.

Having broached the subject, Roarke quickly regained his composure. 'I want you to attend the wedding with me,' he repeated.

She had that part; it was the other she took exception to. 'As your lover?'

Roarke hastily held up a hand to forestall the protests he knew were hovering on her lips. 'I didn't mean that the way it sounded. I need you to *pretend* to be my lover.'

Ginny felt as if she were gaping at him like a fish, her mouth opening and closing repeatedly but nothing coming out. She shut her mouth with a snap of teeth and took a steadying breath. 'You have to be joking!'

'I only wish I were. Believe me, I wouldn't be doing it if it wasn't important.'

Instinctively she knew that was true. Neither would seek help from the other unless business was involved. But what he was asking was out of the question. 'What about what's-her-name, the brunette you're dating? Why don't you ask her to help?' That would be the ideal solution.

The question had him grinding his teeth again. 'She was going to go with me, but as we are no longer an item, I'm left without a partner.'

Ginny stared at him, aware that there was a story he wasn't telling her, and he wasn't going to get away with keeping it to himself if he wanted her help. Not that she was promising anything. 'What happened?'

Roarke's fingers tapped out an irritated tattoo on the desktop. 'She informed me at lunch that her stars told her the weekend was a bad time to travel, so she wouldn't be going. I told her only an idiot would believe such rubbish.'

Ginny winced. 'Bad move,' she pronounced sympathetically and he grimaced.

'Tell me about it! The upshot was she took offence. Apparently, her stars also said it was a good time to end relationships that were going nowhere.'

'Oh, dear!' Ginny commiserated, biting back a laugh.

Sensing it, he sighed ruefully. 'I know, I know. Things went from bad to worse. Which brings me to you. Will you help me out?'

'Why me?' Ginny asked, spreading her hands questioningly. 'Why not ask one of those women who aren't in the little black book you haven't got?'

She got some idea how serious the situation was when she didn't get a smart comeback to her remark. 'Because most of them are known to the family, and I need someone who is a complete stranger. Grandfather won't be there and he's the only person that knows you.'

'Now, that you've simply got to explain,' she insisted.

His reluctance was palpable. 'It's complicated. There are…family complications.'

Family complications covered a multitude of sins, as she knew only too well. As an explanation, it fell way short of the mark. 'You're going to have to come up with a better reason than that if I'm to help you,' she declared bluntly, and his eyes snapped to hers.

'Does this mean you're going to do it?' he wanted to know.

Ginny shrugged, kicking herself for the slip. 'It means I'm thinking about it,' she conceded. Families were a touchy subject. Her inclination, due to her own experience, was to help if an injustice was being done, but otherwise she preferred to keep out of it. Roarke was going to have to do some fancy talking. 'Just tell me, Roarke. Whatever you say, and whatever my decision, nothing is going to go outside this room.'

He looked at her for so long a time she thought he would refuse, but then he nodded. 'OK, listen up. My latest stepmother's name is Jenna. When she was still my father's fiancée, she thought it would be fun to make it with father and son. To put it bluntly, she did her best to seduce me. Contrary to your beliefs, I don't sleep with every woman I meet. I especially do not get involved with those attached to my own family. Jenna did not take kindly to my refusal to play the game with her. She went running to my father with the tale that I had tried to force myself on her. Naturally, I denied it, but my father has always been jealous of his women, and he chose to believe her rather than me. The consequence was that he refused to talk to me for the better part of three years.

'We are back on speaking terms now, but the relationship is still fragile. Which brings me to the problem. When I visited him recently on his birthday, Jenna started getting up to her old tricks again. I managed to fend her off without upsetting my father, but I know how she works. If I turn up alone, she'll try again, and heaven alone knows what my refusal will lead to this time.'

Ginny studied his grim face and sympathised with his dilemma. 'Perhaps if you were to go to your father first, this time he would react differently,' she proposed, without any real expectation of that happening. Her own experience with her father had taught her that they didn't change that easily.

Roarke grimaced. 'I thought about it, but I can't take the risk. I decided my best option was to arrive with a woman on my arm. That way Jenna will have to keep her distance.'

'And if she doesn't, I'll be there to ward her off?' she murmured, following his line of thought easily. Roarke looked at her sharply.

'*Will* you be there?'

Ginny glanced down at her hands. Though he didn't know it, he had her. When it came to families she had her own vulnerabilities, which made it virtually impossible for her to walk away from helping someone else. She didn't want what had happened to her to happen to Roarke, whether she liked him or not.

'I must be crazy to even consider it,' she sighed as she raised her head.

'But you'll do it?' he urged hopefully, and she rolled her eyes.

'Yes, I'll do it,' Ginny confirmed, and was instantly consumed by doubts. But it was too late to back out. She had given her word, and it was a matter of honour with her that she kept it. Ever since the man she had trusted had abandoned her after making all sorts of promises, she had vowed that any she made she would keep, no matter what.

Roarke's famous smile appeared, but there was no glitter of satisfaction in his eyes at having won her over, only gratitude. 'Thank you, Ginny. You've probably no idea what you've done, but you've just saved my relationship with my father from total meltdown.'

She understood better than he thought, but that was another story. 'Just remember you owe me one.' She dismissed his thanks uncomfortably. 'So, what time is the wedding, and how are we getting there?'

'Saturday afternoon, so if we fly out Friday evening, we'll have some time to settle in before the ceremony,' Roarke obliged, sending a shock wave through her.

'Fly out? What do you mean, fly out?' she demanded

to know, sitting up straighter. 'Just where is this wedding taking place?'

'Switzerland. Lake Constance, to be exact. At my mother's summer residence. You'll like it there,' he declared confidently.

Ginny ignored that last point and concentrated on the first. 'Switzerland! Damn you, Roarke Adams, you said nothing about the wedding taking place abroad. You know darn well I thought it was in this country!' she remonstrated with him.

Now there was a gleam in his eye as he grinned at her. 'I thought you'd refuse to go if you knew.'

Ginny ground her teeth helplessly. She might well have refused, but the die was cast. She had given her word and that was that. Getting to her feet, she glowered down at him. 'You are an impossible man. You don't just owe me, you owe me big time,' she pronounced, then promptly spun on her heel and headed for the door.

'Ask for anything you like, and it's yours,' Roarke called after her.

She halted but didn't turn round. 'Anything?'

'Just name it.'

A catlike smile curved her lips. 'Very well, I'll get back to you when I've made up my mind,' she agreed, closing the door behind her. Roarke Adams was about to find out her help didn't come cheap.

CHAPTER TWO

GINNY went out to dinner with Daniel that evening. She liked him a lot, but it wasn't always easy to enjoy his conversations, because he could be rather stuffy. He could also, though it pained her to admit it, be something of the cold fish Roarke thought him. Tonight, though, she had to work extra hard to concentrate whilst he told her about his terrible day. Unfortunately, Ginny's thoughts were miles away, and that irritated her, because she didn't like the fact that Roarke kept floating into her mind. Thankfully, Daniel didn't appear to notice her distraction, and she made a concerted effort to be more attentive whilst they waited for their desserts.

When Daniel reached across the table and took her hand, she smiled at him just a little curiously, because he wasn't a 'touching' sort of person.

'I have a surprise for you,' he declared with boyish enthusiasm, and Ginny's heart suddenly leapt into her throat as she wondered if this was to be the moment he proposed.

'You have?' she asked a tad breathlessly, whilst mentally she prepared herself for what she would say in response. The surroundings could have been more romantic—the restaurant was chosen for its convenience, not its ambience. 'What sort of surprise?'

Daniel's smile broadened at her apparent eagerness. 'My parents have invited us both to their place for the weekend. When I told them how wonderful you are, my mother insisted that she had to meet you. I know she'll adore you as much as I do.'

Ginny tried her best to hold on to her smile, but she could feel it fading and her facial muscles stiffening. It wasn't that it hadn't been the question she had hoped for, but rather the fact she was going to have to refuse what was close to being a royal summons.

'Oh, Daniel, I'm so sorry, but I can't go. I was going to tell you later. I have to go to Switzerland this weekend,' she told him apologetically, hoping to soften the blow, but she could tell from the way he dropped her hand that he was not best pleased.

'With Adams, I presume!' Daniel responded frostily, causing her to blink at his tone.

Ever since she had agreed to this trip, Ginny had been wondering what she was going to tell Daniel. She abhorred deception, but his reaction told her clearly that the truth was out of the question. She had known for a long time that Roarke didn't think highly of Daniel, but she hadn't realised until now just how deeply Daniel disliked Roarke.

'Of course. It's business,' she lied, watching him sit back and fold his arms.

'I don't trust him,' Daniel pronounced bluntly, and Ginny frowned just a little. She could see where this was going, but she had never given him cause to worry. It surprised her to think he had given the possibility credence. He had no need to be jealous.

'You trust *me*, don't you?' she asked soothingly, and he instantly reached for her hand again.

'I do. Of course I do. It's just that that man…' Daniel let the sentence hang, and she knew what he meant. Roarke's reputation went before him.

She squeezed his hand. 'Is someone I have no interest

in at all. However, the trips are part of my job.' OK, not this one, but he didn't need to know that.

Daniel nodded reluctantly. 'I know, but Mother won't be best pleased. She hates having her arrangements altered. She won't like it, and I need her to like you.'

Ginny did a swift mental double-take. Daniel made the visit sound as if she was being presented for inspection, and whether or not he married her depended on his mother's report. She didn't much care for the sound of that, for good reason. Her father had insisted on vetting her boyfriends, and for the most part had found them wanting. They had not been welcome in his house and she had been compelled to follow his dictates until she was old enough not to need his approval.

To find herself on the receiving end of a similar situation now, when she had put all that behind her, made the hairs on the back of her neck stand up. There was no way she was prepared to go through that.

'Does it really matter if she likes me, Daniel? After all, I'm going out with you, not her.' She tried to make light of it, seeking reassurance.

She got it—of a sort. 'I suppose not,' he agreed uncomfortably, then laughed. 'No, no, of course it doesn't. Though I would prefer her to like you. There's no reason why she shouldn't, of course. It's simply that I've always sought her opinion on the important things,' Daniel explained, as if that would make it acceptable.

Ginny swallowed her unease. The situations weren't the same. All she would be doing was meeting his parents. It had to happen eventually. 'I shall do my best to make her like me, if that will make you happy. All we have to do is postpone the visit for a few weeks.' If it was important to him, then she would bite the bullet. As he said, there was no reason why his mother shouldn't like her. She shouldn't allow the past to cloud the present.

Daniel looked relieved. 'That would be wonderful. I just know she's going to like you. My mother has a very discerning eye.'

Ginny let the matter rest there, but later, when she was lying in her bed trying to sleep, the conversation went over and over in her mind. An uncomfortable feeling of *déjà vu* came over her. Daniel was the man she'd settled for, but she didn't want to have to battle his mother for him, and that was what she feared was going to happen. She had been through that, and wasn't about to let it happen again. But maybe she was seeing bogeymen where there were none. After all, she was predisposed to balk at the idea of being inspected. It would be best to reserve judgement until she had met his parents.

They couldn't be as bad as her own. Nobody's could. With which comforting thought she was finally able to drift off to sleep.

The rest of the week was hectic, and Friday came round all too quickly. As she packed for the trip that evening, Ginny decided she was out of her mind. Not only had she bought a new outfit for the occasion, which would have been acceptable, but she had bought several other things as well. For a trip she hadn't wanted to go on, and certainly wasn't looking forward to. The truth of the matter was that she couldn't just turn out in any old rag. Never mind she was going to be playing a part, these people were Roarke's family, and a wedding was a very special occasion. She couldn't bring any sort of disharmony to the day by treating it as a non-event. Besides, she had the feeling Jenna Adams would be dressed in only the best, and there was no way she would let the woman upstage her.

A glance at her watch told Ginny that Roarke would be here soon. Closing the case, she took it out to the hall, then double-checked that she had her passport in her handbag. Which left her with nothing to do but wait, and nerves started to churn in her stomach. They had nothing to do with flying, because she was well used to it. Nor was it due to the fact that she was travelling with Roarke, for she had done that countless times too. No, the nerves were due to the fact she hated waiting. Waiting gave her time to think, and her thoughts were rarely pleasant.

She had learned to keep herself busy, to always have something on hand in which to engross herself, but she couldn't do that now because Roarke was due any minute. She paced to the window of her flat and stared down at the road, but no car was pulling up. Where was he?

The silent question triggered a memory, and she could see herself looking out of the window of that grotty bedsit, waiting for Mark to come home so she could tell him her news. He had never come. Instead he had abandoned her to a terrifying future which had ultimately led to tragedy. She had waited that night, too. Alone in the dark, in pain.

'No!' With a low moan Ginny spun round, closing out the thoughts. She wouldn't go there. Not again.

The sound of the intercom buzzing made her jump, but it was closely followed by a sense of relief. He was here. She crossed to the intercom.

'Hello?'

'It's Roarke,' his disembodied voice informed her.

'Top floor, on the right,' she directed him, pressing the door release. She just had time to catch him muttering, 'It would be, wouldn't it!'

Ginny went to the door to meet him. To her eyes he didn't look the least bit out of breath when he reached her.

'Hasn't anyone ever thought of installing a lift?' he complained, and she shook her head at him.

'It's only three floors.'

'But six flights,' he was quick to point out.

'Quit complaining. You're the fittest man I know,' Ginny responded dryly. She knew for a fact that he worked out regularly, and though she had never seen it, she suspected there wasn't a spare ounce of flesh on the whole of his body.

'Remind me never to come to you for sympathy,' Roarke muttered as he glanced around. 'Is this it?' he asked, pointing to her single case.

Ginny nodded. 'It's all I shall need for a few days,' she confirmed, though she was well aware she had packed too much.

Roarke hefted her case and laughed. 'My mother never travels with less than thirty pieces of luggage.'

Ginny couldn't imagine having the clothes to fill them. 'Think about the excess she must have to pay!' she exclaimed in amazement.

'Think of the pandemonium that arises every time she thinks a piece is missing!' Roarke countered sardonically, and Ginny winced.

'Ouch. Does that happen often?'

'Nearly every time. You see, life has to be a drama for her. She's the prima donna to end all prima donnas. It wouldn't surprise me if my sister is marrying this man just to get away from our mother,' he declared outrageously.

'Oh, but surely she loves him,' Ginny protested, uneasy at the idea that any woman would do such a thing.

Roarke shrugged indifferently. 'She probably thinks she does.'

'Thinks she does?' Ginny challenged as she pulled the door closed behind her and checked it was securely shut.

Roarke started down the stairs. 'Caroline is very much like our mother. She can convince herself of anything. If she wants to get away from Mother's influence, she could well have convinced herself she loves this guy.' He took time out to shoot her a mocking glance over his shoulder. 'You might have gathered that relationships aren't our thing. Caro's a brilliant flautist, but emotionally she's caught in the fallout of our parents' broken relationships like the rest of us. I give this marriage a fifty-fifty chance at best.'

Having reached the ground, Roarke held the door open for her. 'You don't expect it to last?' Ginny asked as she walked outside.

Taking her arm, Roarke guided her to where he had parked his car. 'None of the others have, so the odds are against it.'

'Which is why you aren't even going to attempt a proper marriage,' she pronounced, and Roarke grinned at her over the boot before closing it with a solid thunk.

'Got it in one.'

He helped her into the car, but there was very little time for talking as the traffic that evening was heavier than usual. In fact, they only just made it to the airport in time, and their flight had already been called. Ginny didn't have time to catch a breath until they were in the air and the seat belt sign went out.

'There's nothing like a frantic last-minute dash to set you up for the weekend,' Roarke drawled sardonically as he made himself comfortable in the spacious first class seats.

'I look at it this way, things can only get better,' Ginny responded lightly.

He laughed. 'Don't you believe it. You haven't spent any time with my family before.'

Ginny frowned at him. 'Nobody can be as bad as the picture you're painting,' she argued, though she knew full well that they could be as cold and unforgiving as an arctic winter. 'Your grandfather is always a gentleman.'

'True,' Roarke agreed easily. 'He's one member of the family I'd do anything for. Unfortunately, he won't be there. Pressure of work, he told me, but I think he just doesn't want to run into my mother. They don't see eye to eye on anything.'

The affection in his voice when he spoke of his grandfather caused Ginny to look at him curiously. 'So there's one human being you do care about. You aren't quite the lost cause you like to make out. Why do you hide it?'

Roarke glanced round at her, a mocking smile back on his lips. 'Wait till you meet the family. Then, if you're half as smart as I think you are, you'll understand.'

Ginny looked away, fixing her attention on the view from the window. She wasn't sure she wanted to meet any of his family. Then a small smile tweaked at her lips. Well, they were the *Adams* family, so what else could she expect?

'What's so funny?' Roarke enquired, and Ginny, who hadn't realised she was smiling, hastily composed her features.

'Private joke,' she murmured with a shrug, hoping to put him off asking further, which it did, but only set him off in another unexpected direction.

After giving her a doubtful look, as if he had guessed what she was thinking, he said, 'So what about your family? They can't be as gruesome as mine.'

It was an automatic response for Ginny to tense, though she had battled hard to feel nothing over the years. She tensed because the memories were as painful as they had ever been. Try as she might not to care, she knew in her heart of hearts that she always would.

'I have no family,' she told him shortly, knowing she sounded far too abrupt, which would only pique his irritating interest.

There was a second of surprise while he assimilated this, then he frowned as he made the logical assumption. 'I'm sorry. I had no idea your parents were dead. You must miss them.'

Ginny had no intention of explaining anything to him, but, on the other hand, he was offering sympathy, and she couldn't take that under false pretences either. Caught between a rock and a hard place, she felt compelled to put him straight. 'They're not dead,' she corrected bluntly.

Beside her, Roarke's eyebrows rose, then drew together in another frown. 'You're saying you don't know who they are? That would explain the lack of photographs in your flat.'

Gritting her teeth, Ginny swivelled her head to give him a darkling look. 'I'm not saying that at all. Now, if you don't mind, I'd rather we changed the subject.' She couldn't be more pointed than that, but, as she had expected, Roarke ignored the heavy hint.

'Hey, you can't leave it there. You've got my mind buzzing with off-the-wall scenarios here. Besides, I told you about the skeletons in my family closet, so it's only fair you should do the same,' he cajoled her.

'You volunteered the information,' she was quick to point out. 'I could have done with knowing less.'

Roarke grinned. 'Come on now, sweetheart. You know you found it fascinating in a sort of perverse way.'

'I did not!' she denied, though she knew that wasn't totally true.

'Did too!' he quipped back, making them sound like two children sniping at each other. It made her want to laugh, and she hated that he could do that to her.

She narrowed her eyes at him. 'OK, so I didn't find it completely uninteresting,' she admitted, and held up her hand as he started to speak. 'But that doesn't mean I have to tell you anything about my family.'

'So you do have one. I was beginning to think you sprang into this world fully formed,' he mocked her, and Ginny sighed. He wasn't going to give up unless she said something.

There was no way she could keep the reluctance from her expression, and she wasn't laughing when she spoke. 'I'll tell you one thing, but only if you promise not to ask any more questions.'

The laughter faded from his grey eyes. 'You make it sound like the end of the world.'

She held his gaze. 'Your promise, Roarke.'

'OK, I promise. No more questions, no matter what you say.'

Ginny glanced down at her hands, composing herself so that she would reveal nothing, not by a look or an expression. Her gaze was bland when she looked at him again. 'Very well, I'll tell you this much. I no longer exist,' she told him quietly, and saw the myriad questions forming in his head. Yet she knew he wouldn't let one of them pass his lips, for he had given his word and she knew that, once given, he would not go back on it.

Roarke sat back in his seat, puffing out a frustrated breath. 'You realise this is going to drive me mad?'

That wasn't her intention, for she wasn't deliberately cruel. It had been her only defence to his probing questions. She couldn't tell him that her family wasn't dead to her, but that she was dead to her family. He would want to know why. She had had to shut him up and that had been the only way.

'Best not to think about it, then,' she advised, picking up one of the magazines she had bought to while away the flight with.

'God, you're an aggravating woman! Why didn't you just say nothing?' he demanded testily, and that made her lips quirk.

'I tried that, but you insisted. You only have yourself to blame. Something for you to remember in future. Curiosity can be a dangerous thing,' she told him with a husky laugh.

The sound of her laugh brought a rueful expression to his face. 'You're enjoying this, aren't you?'

Ginny couldn't help but laugh again. 'There's a certain amusement in the situation.'

'I had no idea you could be so nasty.'

She shook her head sadly. 'I told you. You...'

'...only have myself to blame. Thank you for rubbing salt into the wound. It's made me feel a lot better,' Roarke muttered grumpily, but she could tell there was no real animosity in it. He had been well and truly hoist by his own petard.

Secure in the knowledge that she had headed him off at the pass, Ginny concentrated on her magazine until her eyes began to close. Knowing sleep would make the journey pass more quickly, she settled her seat into a more comfortable position and was asleep in seconds.

It was a hand gently shaking her that brought her awake some time later, and in that moment of slight disorientation she glanced round to get her bearings and found herself looking into Roarke's concerned eyes no more than inches away from her own.

'What—?' she croaked, inexplicably fascinated by the depth in those grey orbs. She experienced the fanciful notion that they were bottomless. Perfect for drowning in.

'You were having a bad dream.' Roarke's soft words cut into her errant thoughts, causing her to blink and really see him. The words sent a chill through her and she shivered. 'I thought you'd rather I woke you up.'

Ginny licked her lips and swallowed, suddenly aware of a warmth on her shoulder. Glancing down, she discovered Roarke's hand still rested there from when he had shaken her to rouse her. It was this that was creating the only hot spot on her body, but it was radiating warmth. Disconcerted by the effect, she touched the button which brought her seat upright and removed his hand at the same time.

'Thanks,' she muttered awkwardly. 'Was I making much noise?' she added, glancing round surreptitiously to see if anyone was looking at her. Much to her relief, nobody was.

Only Roarke was studying her with any interest. 'Just whimpering sounds that warned me whatever was happening in that head of yours, it wasn't pleasant. Do you often have bad dreams?'

Glad to hear that she had stopped short of one of her more explosive nightmares, Ginny shook her head. 'Only now and then,' she revealed. Once she had been plagued by them. Driven to the point of exhaustion by nights of broken sleep. Time had seen them fade until now she only dreamed when she was worried or upset. It must have been Roarke's questions about her family which had set her off this time.

She'd been dreaming of the last time she had seen her

family. Her father had been as cold and remorseless as ever. Denying her entry to the house. Saying things in that harsh voice he used to show his disapproval. Things that had cut her pride to ribbons, though she had held her head high. He had seen her off as if she had been a creature from the gutter. But that was what she was to him then. No longer his daughter, just a thing he would step over in the street.

Roarke's hand on her arm gave her a start. 'Don't,' he ordered gently when she looked a query at him. 'Come back. Wherever you just were, you clearly don't want to be there.'

His perceptiveness brought an unexpected lump to her throat, and she had to clear it. 'Some dreams are hard to shake off,' she confessed, and he smiled faintly, as if he knew from experience.

'For some of us the past isn't a pleasant place to be, is it?'

That wasn't a path she wanted to travel, and in order to fend him off Ginny eyed him ironically. 'You have bad dreams? I would have thought you'd need a conscience for that.'

He wagged an admonitory finger at her. 'Now, that wasn't nice, sweetheart. As it happens, I do have a conscience, but I doubt very much if I could convince you of the fact. You have this habit of expecting the worst of me.'

'A side you delight in showing me,' she was quick to point out, and he laughed.

'Ah, well, if you expect to catch fish you have to use the right bait, otherwise they won't rise,' he explained, and Ginny's eyes narrowed.

'Implying that I rise to the bait, I presume?' she charged wrathfully.

'Which you do beautifully.'

She wanted to respond to that with a furious denial, but to do so would be to rise to the lure he had just put out, and therefore confirm what he was saying. She had to satisfy herself with a baleful look and one word.

'Snake.'

Roarke chuckled. 'Damn, but I have to admire your self-control. You are one cool customer.'

She might look cool, but inside Ginny was seething to the point of incandescence with frustration. 'You're too clever by half, Roarke Adams. People like you have been known to come to a sticky end.'

'There, you see, there's something for you to look forward to. My comeuppance. Will you look on, gloating with satisfaction?' he teased her, and she rolled her eyes.

'Oh, please, gloating is so passé. I'll probably be leading the cheering section. It will be made up of all the women you've toyed with over the years.'

'I'm afraid it won't be as large a group as you imagine. I'm on pretty good terms with most of my exes,' he reminded her, and she knew that basically it was true. She might rag him over the ones who had taken it badly, but they were in the minority.

Ginny had never been able to understand it. How could women allow themselves to be used as they were, and still like the man when he decided it was over? 'You must be related to Svengali,' she said now, and Roarke smiled rakishly.

'Sweetheart, I don't have to hypnotise a woman to, as you'd put it, have my wicked way with her.'

'No,' Ginny agreed with a grimace. 'You merely smile at them, and they turn all weak at the knees.'

'What turns you weak at the knees, Ginny? What's Daniel's secret weapon?'

There was no way Ginny would tell him that if Daniel had a secret weapon he kept it well hidden. He didn't turn her weak at the knees, and she wouldn't want him to. She'd done that, and it wasn't all it was cracked up to be. 'That's none of your business.'

Roarke's smile suggested he wasn't taken in by her response, but at least he didn't follow it up. No, he took a different tack. 'So, what did dear Daniel say when you told him where you were going this weekend?'

The nerves in Ginny's body jolted uncomfortably. Picking up her magazine, she flipped it open. 'He said nothing. Why should he have anything to say?' she responded in an offhand manner designed to tell him how unimportant the situation was.

Roarke studied her downbent head curiously. 'You mean he saw nothing odd in you going away with me? How open-minded of him. I didn't think he had it in him, to be frank.'

Ginny shrugged. 'We travel together too often for him to be upset this time,' she offered, recalling with a tiny frown just how upset he had been.

'True, but this is different...or doesn't he know that?' Roarke added thoughtfully, and Ginny groaned silently at his persistence. 'You didn't tell him, did you? Where does he think you are?' The amusement in his voice made her wince.

Slapping the magazine closed, she turned to stare him out. 'This is a business trip as far as he's concerned. When I realised how much he dislikes you, I chose not to tell him. Are you satisfied now? Can I read my magazine in peace?'

'Daniel dislikes me?' he asked, sounding even more amused. 'The man has a hidden depth. Well, well, well.'

Exasperated, Ginny was tempted to hit him with her

magazine. 'It's not uncommon for people to dislike you, Roarke, hard as that is to believe. I dislike you too.'

'Ah, but does he dislike me for the same reason? You see me as a womaniser. Is that what Daniel thinks too?' Roarke mused, then snapped his fingers as an idea struck him. 'Of course, that's it. He's afraid I might turn my attention to you.'

It was irritating that Roarke should hit the nail on the head so quickly. 'I told him he had nothing to worry about. I'm not the least bit interested in you. I think I may even have mentioned a ten-foot bargepole. That desperate I'm not,' she added sardonically for good measure.

'Besides, you have Daniel,' Roarke put in sagaciously.

'Exactly,' Ginny agreed, returning once more to her magazine. 'I have Daniel, and I'm not in the market for anyone else.' Saying which, she turned her shoulder on him and concentrated on the words on the page.

Roarke wasn't to know that they were little more than a jumble of letters because her thoughts were concentrated on those brief moments when a pair of roguish grey eyes had set her nerves skittering and her heart skipping. Why they had become fascinating, she couldn't say, but she was seeing them in a way she never had before. Added to that, she could still feel where his hand had touched her. She was aware of him, too. Physically. Suddenly she could sense him, when she had sat beside him before and never felt a thing. It was as if something had been switched on inside her, and she was far from comfortable with it. She had to be losing it to find Roarke Adams even remotely attractive. That damned chemistry had picked a fine time to rear its ugly head. However, what could be switched on could also be switched off, and that was what she was going to do. All she had to do was will it. She was a sensible person, so it shouldn't be that difficult... should it?

CHAPTER THREE

IT WAS evening when they landed, but as it was summer the sun hadn't quite set and it was still warm. Someone had sent a car to collect them, and Ginny was more than a little surprised to find herself being ushered into a luxury limousine.

'Somebody's pushing the boat out,' she murmured as she ran an appreciative hand over the soft leather seat.

'Mother never travels in less than the best,' Roarke explained dryly as he joined her in the back, having passed a few friendly words with the driver, whom he obviously knew well.

'Hasn't she heard of energy saving?' she charged, judging that the limousine would guzzle petrol as if it was going out of fashion.

Roarke uttered a bark of laughter. 'She never hears anything that would be to her disadvantage. Which is why she insists her children call her Marganita and not mother. The surgeon's skill has maintained her youthful looks, which would be undermined by having a son my age.'

'What do you call her?' Ginny wasn't sure whether the woman sounded likeable or not, he was painting such a dreadful picture of her. Her eyes narrowed. Just a minute, why was he doing that? It wasn't like him at all to be so openly critical. She began to smell a rat.

That roguish smile reappeared. 'Mother, of course. I think it's important somebody keeps her in touch with reality.'

'Why bother if she's such an ogre?' Ginny countered,

definitely getting the idea that something was more than a little fishy here.

'She's my mother. I can't just abandon her,' Roarke replied carelessly, and Ginny knew she was right. She sent him a narrow-eyed look.

'You, Roarke Adams are a twenty-four-carat fraud,' she accused, which had him looking at her with what she could clearly see was feigned surprise.

'I have no idea what you're talking about.'

'Your family is gruesome and your grandfather is the only one you'd give the time of day? Ha! The fact that I'm here gives the lie to that. You care so much for your father you don't want to hurt him, and as for your mother… You love every larger than life inch of her,' Ginny declared roundly, the glow in her eyes daring him to deny it.

One eyebrow quirked. 'Is that so?' he said softly, and she nodded, quirking an eyebrow right back at him.

Roarke glanced away, scratching his ear. When he looked back, his expression was ruefully impressed. 'You aren't just a pretty face and a fabulous pair of legs, are you?'

'I was hired for my brain,' she confirmed, but Roarke smiled.

'And a humdinger of a brain it is, but a mere brain didn't see what you did. How does a woman who's locked up in layers of permafrost get such an accurate insight into man's deeper emotions? Sort of begs the question: were you always as frosty as you are now?'

Ginny gave him a sad look. 'Just because I don't choose to live my life as a high drama like your mother doesn't make me frosty,' she said, and received a look of high scepticism.

'I beg to differ. A glance from those eyes of yours can

deliver a serious case of frostbite,' he drawled humorously.

'The answer to that is to not say anything to provoke me,' she advised, glancing out of the window and enjoying the view as the car began to circle the lake. They must be getting closer to their destination, she decided, and a tiny flutter of nerves started up inside her.

It wasn't that she was really worried, for she was used to meeting new people, and all she had to do was be there to show Roarke's stepmother that he was spoken for. Money for old rope, really. By Sunday evening she would be back in her own home again, and he would owe her one *big* favour.

All the same, the situation was just that little bit different. This was a family function and, Lord knew, she had never been a whizz at those. Doing what was expected of her, for a father who was notoriously hard to please, had been difficult. He had hated her spirit, and had done his best to crush it. That he had failed was due to her inner strength. She had refused to give in, and it had taken her along paths leading to betrayal and rejection. Her determination to be free had cost her dearly, and the memories were painful to this day.

She was distracted from her uncomfortable thoughts by the driver turning the car in through iron gates set in a wall that appeared to stretch for ever. It was a winding drive through natural forest, and Ginny wasn't in the least surprised when they finally came out of the trees and found themselves drawing up before a large turn-of-the-century mansion. The views over the lake were spectacular.

Climbing out of the limousine, Ginny stared up at the impressive frontage. Goodness only knew how many bedrooms there were.

'It's not much to look at, but it's still home to us,' she sighed dramatically.

Roarke slipped his hands into his trouser pockets and rocked back on his heels. 'Impressed?' he queried, tongue-in-cheek.

'I'm impressed by the size of the fuel bills. It must cost a packet to heat this place,' she exclaimed in awe.

He grinned. 'Which is why it's the summer place. Summers are hot, so there's no need to heat it. There's a cool head under all that passion and flamboyance.'

She looked at him speculatively. 'Aha, I'm beginning to see where you get your cunning from. What characteristics did you inherit from your father, other than an eye for the ladies?'

His laughter sent a trickle of pleasure down her spine. 'Why, good looks, charm and wit, of course.'

'Very useful,' she drawled ironically.

'All depends what you want to use them for,' he countered smoothly, and she had no trouble guessing what he meant.

'So, why isn't your father in the hotel business?' Ginny asked as they walked to the front door. Lawns stretched out on either side and were immaculately kept.

Roarke shrugged. 'He's better at spending money than making it. Fortunately, he can never spend what he has. He inherited a tidy fortune from his maternal grandmother, and has been living on the interest ever since. Oh, he isn't a fool where money is concerned. It's all stashed away, making more money than he could spend in three lifetimes, but it means he doesn't have to work.'

'So what does he do all day?' Ginny wanted to know, frowning up at him in disapproval.

Seeing the look on her face, Roarke quirked an eyebrow

mischievously. 'I told you, he spends money,' he said mildly, just as the door opened as if by magic.

Ginny had been going to pursue the subject, but the vision before her took the words out of her mouth. Standing deferentially in the doorway was a butler. Not just any butler, but a genuine English one from the way he wished them good evening. He could have stepped right out of that well-known series of humorous novels.

Roarke stooped down to whisper in her ear. 'If the wind changes, you'll stay like that,' he said and, realising she was staring with her mouth open, Ginny closed it with a snap of teeth.

'Is he real?' she asked, stepping inside in response to Roarke's hand in the small of her back.

'The lady wants to know if you're real, Watson,' Roarke promptly addressed the question to the butler, much to Ginny's discomfort.

'Indeed I am, sir,' Watson replied with gravity, but Ginny thought she caught the faintest of twinkles in his eyes.

'He's real,' Roarke reported back, and Ginny sent him a look sharp enough to slay him where he stood.

'Very funny,' she growled, then gave the butler a friendly smile. 'Take no notice of him, Watson. He has a warped sense of humour.'

'Mr Roarke's foibles are well known to me, miss.'

Laughing, Roarke turned back to the butler. 'Are we the last to arrive?'

'Of those expected today, yes, sir. Madam had dinner put back to coincide with your arrival. Cocktails will be served in the drawing room in half an hour.'

Roarke glanced at his watch. 'We can make that. There's no need to show us up, I know the way.'

Watson inclined his head in assent. 'Very good, sir. I'll have Carl bring your luggage up directly.'

The staircase was beautifully carved in wood and, climbing up it, Ginny could imagine elegant *fin de siècle* ladies swaying down it in their waspwaisted dresses, bent on making a spectacular entrance.

'Has Watson been with your family long?' The man was clearly somewhere around retirement age, but he still had a straight back and a full head of silvery-grey hair.

'Since I was a boy. He's had to rescue me from more scrapes than I care to remember,' Roarke enlightened her as he ushered her down one corridor, then left into another. It was very confusing.

'Could you draw me a map. I think I could get lost in here,' Ginny declared wryly. 'Has anyone disappeared never to be seen again?'

'Not recently,' he responded with a teasing grin. 'Here we are.' Stopping by a door, he opened it and pushed it wide.

It was a beautiful room, with a double bed at one end and a sitting area complete with couch and armchairs encircling a fireplace at the other. There were two large windows opposite, one giving access to a balcony, and Ginny went to look out, delighted to realise it offered a grand view of the lake. She decided she would be very comfortable here.

Turning, she found Roarke had followed her in. 'Like it?' He sought her approval, and she nodded, walking past him to take hold of the door.

'It's absolutely perfect. Now, if you wouldn't mind leaving, I would like to clean up before dinner.' She stared at him, urging him to go, and noticed that Roarke looked oddly discomfited.

'I would, but there's a problem,' he said uneasily.

Her eyes narrowed. 'Problem?'

He winced. 'Something I forgot to tell you.'

Feeling uneasy herself now, Ginny was about to ask what it was when a figure appeared in the doorway. He was carrying their bags, so she identified him as Carl. What she didn't expect was that he would deposit all the luggage on the chest at the foot of the bed and leave again, as quietly as he had arrived. Understanding was swift, and Ginny looked up at Roarke with eyes that registered first surprise, then anger. She let the door go in order to point an accusing finger at him.

'If you think for one minute that I am going to—' The words were abruptly cut off as Roarke closed the gap between them in no time and clamped one hand over her mouth and used the other to swing her away from the door, which he shut with a flick of his foot.

'For the love of Mike, keep your voice down,' he ordered in an urgent undertone, whilst Ginny glared at him over his hand.

'Take your hands off me!' she ordered, sounding both angry and garbled.

'What?' Roarke asked absently, intent on listening for sounds outside the now closed door.

Ginny chose a more direct method of communication, and the business end of her heel connected with his shin.

'Ow!' he exclaimed, releasing her to rub at the damaged area.

Stepping out of reach, Ginny folded her arms wrathfully. 'I said, take your hands off me,' she repeated for his benefit, and Roarke straightened up. 'Why didn't you tell me we would be sharing a room?' she demanded to know.

'Because I forgot,' he growled back.

She laughed incredulously. 'You forgot? You can't seriously expect me to believe that?'

Grey eyes glowered at her. 'Right now, I don't care what the hell you believe. The truth is I forgot. I use this room when I'm alone or when I'm not, and you aren't the one I was supposed to be with. The arrangements were made ages ago, remember?'

Some of the initial anger drained out of her at his explanation, but that didn't mean she was happy with the situation. 'OK, you forgot, but that doesn't mean I intend to share this room with you, Roarke.'

Satisfied that there was no serious damage, Roarke abandoned his examination of his shin and gave her a blunt look. 'You're going to have to.'

That set her nostrils flaring. 'I don't have to do anything!' she declared, bringing a mocking smile to his lips.

'The woman in my life shares my room, and so far as this family is concerned you are the woman in my life. Get used to it. You're staying here.'

Ginny would have given anything to be able to counter his argument, but she could not. She had agreed to play a part, and apparently that meant sharing this room with him. That being the case, she was going to lay down some ground rules right now.

'OK, so we share the room. We don't share the bed. You can sleep on the couch,' she ordered coldly, and that brought a glint of amusement back to his eyes.

'Sure you don't want me to sleep in the bath?' he mocked, and she returned the smile with saccharine.

'Don't tempt me!' she threatened, and went across to the bed to pick up her case. 'Before I get changed, is there anything else you've forgotten and would care to tell me about?'

He shrugged, hands busying themselves with the buttons of his jacket, which he removed and tossed on to the bed along with his tie. 'Nothing springs to mind,' he declared, starting on the buttons of his shirt.

Ginny found herself staring as if hypnotised. For reasons she couldn't afterwards explain, she couldn't seem to take her eyes off the movement of his fingers. It was only when they paused near his waist that she blinked and looked up—to find him watching her with a wicked glint in his eye.

'Want to help?' he invited in an ever so slightly husky voice.

Realising what she had been doing, and how it would be perceived, Ginny felt a wave of heat storm into her cheeks. 'You've been undressing yourself long enough to know what you're doing,' she responded tautly, swinging on her heel and heading for the nearest door.

Opening it, she came to a halt. It wasn't the bathroom. She closed her eyes, waiting for the remark that was bound to follow. He didn't keep her waiting long.

'You can use my dressing-room if you like, but yours is the other side of the bed, and the bathroom is to the right of the fire,' Roarke said in that friendly, helpful way that made her want to commit serious bodily harm.

Bracing herself, Ginny turned and met eyes dancing with amusement. 'Thank you,' she gritted out through her teeth, and followed his directions to the other side of the room. Once safely inside the bathroom, she shot the bolt and leant back weakly against the door.

Oh, God, she had just made a complete and utter fool of herself. And why? Because she had been unnerved by finding she had been staring at him whilst he began to undress! What on earth had made her do that? She groaned aloud. He would never let her live it down. She just knew in her bones that he would be throwing it in her face from now till kingdom come.

To cap it all, she was having to share the room with him. Sometimes life was darned unfair. Thank goodness she had thought to bring a robe with her, for, although it was made of some silky material, it covered her from neck to toe. She wouldn't have to swan around in next to nothing in front of him.

With that grateful thought, Ginny set her case down on top of the laundry basket and drew out the two-piece she would wear that night. It didn't take her long to wash off the dust of travel and refresh her make-up, then slip on her stockings and shoes. Finally, she reached for the two-piece. The skirt was simple, black and clingy, whilst the top had a beadwork pattern all over it that glittered in the light and was held up by two thin straps. Ginny had a feeling that Roarke's mother always dressed for dinner, so the evening wear would not be out of place. She ran a brush through her hair, gathered up her belongings and let herself back into the bedroom.

Roarke was already dressed in a dinner suit, and Ginny was compelled to acknowledge once again that she'd rarely seen a man who looked better formally dressed. Probably because he was at home in formal clothes. Mind you, she also had the idea that he would look equally good in informal clothes. Because if Roarke Adams was nothing else, he was a man who was comfortable with who and what he was. It was probably one of the main reasons he was so attractive to women. Women always appeared to go for men who were sure of themselves. Roarke had...the only phrase that really said it all was that old one—*savoir-faire*.

He turned at the sound of her return, and a slow smile spread across his face. 'Very nice. I've always said it, you know how to wear clothes, sweetheart,' he complimented her, which, as it was virtually what she had been thinking about him, made her feel a little strange inside.

Setting her case on the nearest chair, Ginny smoothed away invisible creases from her skirt. 'You didn't say, but it seemed to me, if your mother has a butler she must dine formally.'

'Right down to the napkins and finger bowls,' he confirmed ironically. Then, seeing her sceptical expression, he amended the statement. 'OK, so the finger bowls are a slight exaggeration, but you get the picture.'

Ginny shook her head at him in mild exasperation. 'You enjoy painting your family as a bunch of wildly eccentric loonies, don't you?'

'Makes it less of a shock when you finally get to meet them,' he replied with a chuckle.

She rolled her eyes. 'I'm beginning to believe half of what you say isn't true, and the rest is just plain lies.'

His lips twitched and he quirked an eyebrow at her. 'So, you think you're getting to know me, do you?'

Ginny folded her arms, and tipped her chin challengingly. 'A little. About your family. I said you were a fraud, and nothing has changed my mind since.'

'Hmm,' Roarke mused just as a soft knock came on the door. They looked at each other questioningly, both wondering if this was where the real deception would begin. Bracing himself, Roarke went to the door and opened it.

Immediately the room was pervaded by the scent of Opium. For a moment all Ginny could see was Roarke's back, and then two arms slinked their way around his neck, causing her eyes to widen in surprise.

'Roarke, darling, Watson told me you were here, and I

just had to come and say hello,' a sultry voice declared, and the hairs on the back of Ginny's neck rose.

Ginny watched silently as Roarke attempted to back away, but, tentacle-like, the arms closed around him, drawing him in. She saw Roarke's hands fasten on those arms, trying to dislodge them, but the woman they belonged to wasn't about to let go. Ginny didn't like that one little bit, but didn't have time to analyse why.

Crossing to the door, she pulled it open wider to reveal Roarke and the sexy blue-eyed blonde who had him in her feline grasp. There was no doubt in Ginny's mind that this could only be Jenna Adams. In which case, she had a job to do.

'Hello,' she said mildly, though someone who knew her better would have been uneasy at the glitter in the back of her eyes. Reaching up, Ginny took hold of one of the woman's wrists. 'Let me help you. You seem to have got caught up on something that doesn't belong to you,' she said with a smile that belied the strength with which she pulled the woman's arm down. There was no harm in letting the other woman believe she was fiercely territorial. It was, after all, what Roarke wanted.

Taken by surprise, Jenna Adams gasped and took a hasty step backwards, releasing Roarke, who took the opportunity to put some distance between them.

Warming to her theme, Ginny slipped her arm through Roarke's proprietorially, and kept smiling at the other woman. 'You really should be careful who you get snagged on, Mrs Adams.'

Jenna might have been temporarily knocked off her stride, but she was not the sort of woman to remain so for long. She rallied instantly, looked Ginny up and down, then tossed her head dismissively. 'And you are?' she asked disdainfully, which made Ginny's lips twitch.

'Ginny Harte,' Ginny introduced herself, holding out her hand.

Jenna deigned to touch it briefly. 'You must be Roarke's latest,' she said snidely, but that only got Ginny's dander up. It wasn't often that she took an instant dislike to anyone, but she was willing to make an exception for Jenna Adams. The woman was trouble with a capital T. She had been poured into a glittery red dress that clung to every curve lovingly, leaving little to the imagination.

'That's right,' she said brightly. 'And you're Jenna... his father's wife.'

The reminder caused Jenna to flash her eyes at Ginny, sizing her up as she realised Ginny was possibly a force to be reckoned with. 'Roarke, darling, she sounds positively possessive. I'd be careful, or she'll be putting a ring through your nose before you know it,' she teased with a gurgling laugh, but she was far from amused.

Roarke smiled faintly and covered Ginny's hand with his own. 'I'll take my chances.'

Jenna's lips parted in surprise, and the flash in her eyes became almost feral as she looked from one to the other. 'My, my, she must have something all your other women didn't.'

Roarke glanced down at Ginny, and secretly winked at her. 'She certainly does,' he agreed with feeling, and Ginny almost laughed because she knew what he meant and Jenna didn't.

Jenna took a deep breath, which put her dress under great strain. 'Do let us into the secret. What has she got that the others don't?'

Ginny looked her squarely in the eye. 'Well, for one thing, I don't have a husband,' she said with the precision of a master swordsman, not caring if she offended the other woman or not. It was plain as the nose on her face that Jenna wouldn't like any woman Roarke had. She wanted him for herself.

In response, Jenna laughed grimly. 'Darling, don't think you've almost got one yourself. Roarke isn't going to marry you. He isn't the marrying kind,' she warned, no holds barred.

The statement hung on the air, destined never to be countered, for, as if on cue, a male voice called out from further along the corridor.

'Ah, there you are, Jenna,' Lewis Adams exclaimed. 'I thought you were going to wait for me,' he added just a little testily as he came level with the doorway.

Quick as a flash, Jenna smiled lovingly at the older man and slipped her arm through his. 'Sorry, darling, but I just had to come and say hello to Roarke and his latest lady friend.'

There was a moment when Lewis Adams did not look best pleased, but then he smiled at his son, and Ginny believed she could see genuine warmth there. 'Good to see you, Roarke. And you, too…' He smiled at Ginny and she could see where Roarke had got his charm.

'Ginny,' Roarke introduced her, and Ginny found her hand swallowed in a firm male one.

'Hope you enjoy your stay here, young lady. Now, we'd better get downstairs before your mother pitches a fit,' he added with a significant glance at his son. 'She's been in diva mode since this morning.'

Roarke urged Ginny out of their room ahead of him. 'Never let it be said she missed an opportunity, Dad,' he responded to his father, who was leading the way with his wife sashaying on his arm.

Ginny attempted to remove her hand from Roarke's arm, now that the need for it was past, but he quickly closed a hand over hers again, and when she glanced up he shook his head. Which was just as well, for Jenna looked round then, and would have thought it odd for Ginny not to be clinging to Roarke. She subsided, but holding Roarke's arm was a completely new experience, and she found herself becoming aware of his strength. He was a powerful man in both senses of the word, yet there was nothing threatening about the strength of his body. In fact, for some weird reason, being this close, far from making her uneasy, was strangely comforting. Not a word she would usually use in connection with Roarke, but it certainly made it easier to resign herself to having to remain in close contact with him, at least for the moment.

'Marganita always has to be the centre of attention!' Jenna said irritably, and Ginny guessed she preferred to hold that position.

'She can act how she wants in her own home,' Roarke put in ironically.

'That's what I keep telling you, Jenna,' Lewis told his wife.

'Well, I don't like it,' Jenna complained with a toss of her head.

'You knew how it would be. You didn't have to come, but you insisted, so quit complaining,' her husband advised with a touch of asperity, and Ginny's brows rose thoughtfully.

It seemed to her that Lewis Adams was not as uncritical of his wife as Roarke assumed. Which might suggest that he was beginning to see how wrong he had been. She hoped so, for Roarke's sake.

Back downstairs, they made their way to the drawing room, which opened on to a terrace overlooking the lake. The daylight was fading fast now, and through the opening Ginny could see lights beginning to flicker on in the houses over the water. The room itself was ablaze with light from two elaborate crystal chandeliers, which were reflected back from strategically placed mirrors, and was full of people making quite an incredible amount of noise.

'Mother appears to have invited the whole family to dinner,' Roarke murmured in her ear, and Ginny thought he was probably right.

She was aware that they were drawing some attention. No doubt Roarke's family were speculating as to who she was—and how long she would last. Ginny relaxed, secure in the knowledge that she knew there was nothing between them, and that the 'relationship' would be over in something like forty-eight hours.

'Your family are wondering who I am,' she remarked to Roarke as they ventured further into the room.

'Do you mind being the centre of attention?' he asked, attracting the eye of a passing waiter and handing her a glass of champagne before taking one for himself.

Ginny sipped at the drink and found it a little too dry for her taste. 'Actually, it's quite amusing. If they only knew! In different circumstances, you and I wouldn't come any closer than a ten-foot bargepole would allow. The sad thing is, when you turn up next time with someone else, they won't be the least bit surprised.'

Roarke shrugged that off easily. 'I try not to disappoint them. Ah, I think Mother is holding court over there.' He nodded in the direction of the far end of the room. 'We'd better go and say hello. Brace yourself.'

Ginny felt her stomach lurch. Brace herself for what? She soon found out.

When Marganita Toscari—she always preferred to be known by her maiden name—saw her eldest son making his way towards her through the crowd of guests, she let out a cry and jumped up from her seat to envelop him in a bruising hug. She broke into a veritable spout of Italian, which Ginny found hard to follow, but which Roarke responded to in the same language.

Only when she finally held him at arms' length, did she return to English. 'Roarke, you are a rogue. I may never forgive you for not coming to visit me for months and months. What have you got to say for yourself, you devil?' She didn't wait for his answer, for she caught sight of Ginny hovering behind him and let out another cry, albeit softer. 'Is this your young lady? But she's beautiful, Roarke. Why didn't you tell me how beautiful she was? Introduce us. I insist,' she urged her son, all the time beaming at Ginny, who was beginning to feel uncomfortable at all the attention.

'Ginny, this is my mother. Mother, meet Ginny Harte,' Roarke dutifully obliged, and Ginny just caught the faint gleam in his eye as he took her glass from her before she was overwhelmed by an embrace almost as effusive as the one Marganita had given her son just minutes before.

'Ginny, *cara*, I'm so happy to meet you. Come, give me a hug, for any friend of my son's is welcome here.'

Marganita was a large lady, along the lines of the older sopranos, and hugging her was no easy matter. Ginny did her best, and surfaced pink-cheeked and flustered.

'I'm pleased to meet you, Miss Toscari,' she returned the greeting politely.

The older woman waved her hands and shook her head. 'Marganita. You must call me Marganita, and I shall call you Ginny.'

It was more of a royal pronouncement than a suggestion and Ginny, getting over the shock, smiled. 'Marganita, then.'

'And we shall be friends, and you shall tell me all about yourself. Only not yet. Don't go away, Roarke, there's

someone I want you to meet.' Without further ado,
Marganita scanned the room with the eye of an expert and
set off in search of her quarry.

Grinning, Roarke handed Ginny her glass, and she took
a much needed drink. 'My goodness, is she always so…
so…?' Words failed her.

Roarke laughed affectionately. 'I thought she was re-
markably restrained. As a rule, she can be quite voluble.
I expect it's because her soon to be in-laws are present.
She's making an extra effort so as not to scare them off.'

Ginny pulled a face. 'I think she's probably easier to
get along with in small doses.'

'That's the consensus of opinion of all her children.
Otherwise, she'll try to take over our lives—with the best
of intentions, of course. My father finds it easier to get
along with her now that they aren't actually married,'
Roarke explained.

'Roarke, *caro*.' Marganita's mellifluous tones drew
their attention, and they both turned towards her. She was
smiling broadly and trailing a rather disgruntled man in
her wake.

Ginny took one look at that stern face, and her blood
turned to ice. No! It couldn't be, she told herself, and yet
she knew that it was. Walking towards her was the man
she had thought she would never see again, and had been
comforted by that thought. That man was none other than
her own father. Shock held her to the spot, and she was
sure the colour must have drained from her face.

All she could think was: what was he doing here?

Of all the people it was possible for her to run into, her
father had never been on the list. They didn't inhabit the
same world any more. Yet he was here, and any second
now he was going to see her. She didn't know what he
would do, but instinct told her it would not be good. He

had made his position very clear. So far as he was concerned, she did not exist. Tensing, her heart starting to beat faster, she waited for the moment when he would notice her and recognition would come. Unknowingly, she tightened her hand about the stem of her glass.

'Mother,' Roarke was saying beside her, but Ginny couldn't take her eyes off the man who had come to a halt beside Marganita and who looked first at Roarke and then at her.

Recognition was as instantaneous for him as it had been for her. His reaction was also typical. Drawing himself up, his expression tightened and his face grew red with anger and distaste. If Ginny had held any hope that he might have softened his stance with the passing years, she would have been left in no doubt. That look said it all. He despised her now as much as he had ever done. Only the dictates of good manners stopped him from turning his back and walking away. After that initial moment he kept his gaze firmly averted from her.

It shouldn't have hurt. After all this time, his displeasure should have left her cold, and yet it didn't. Hate him though she might, for what he had done, he still had the power to wound her with his disdain. Yet she was stronger now. Tougher. She wasn't about to turn and run. He might not want to see her, but he had no option. He would be forced to recognise her, and that brought her chin up.

Marganita was still making the introductions. 'Roarke, this is Brigadier Sir Martin Beavis. Caroline is marrying his son, James. Sir Martin, this is my son, Roarke Adams.'

Ginny's breath caught in a tiny gasp when she heard that. Roarke's sister was marrying James? Her heart leapt into her throat. That meant her family were here. Eagerly, she began to look around her, searching for those familiar figures of her mother, brother and sister.

'Pleased to meet you, Sir Martin.' From a long way away she heard Roarke's response, but she was diligently scanning the crowd.

Try as she might, she couldn't see them, and was so intent on what she was doing that Roarke's hand on her arm made her jump. 'Sorry, did you say something?' she asked, glancing round unwillingly. She wanted to find her family before her father knew what she was doing, for he would prevent it by any means.

A tiny frown appeared between his brows at her abstraction. 'I wanted to introduce you to Caroline's future father-in-law,' he said. 'Sir Martin, this is a good friend of mine, Ginny Harte.'

Ginny had no trouble reading the look in her father's eyes. He interpreted 'friend' as 'lover', and made his judgement. In his eyes, she hadn't changed, and that made her so angry. She knew he didn't want to have anything to do with her, but right here he had no option, and she was determined to make him speak.

Raising her chin, she held out her hand. 'Brigadier,' she said challengingly, and knew he was caught by his own notion of what was good manners. He was forced to shake her hand. 'It's been a long time. You haven't changed.' She had always called him Brigadier, for he treated his family as if they were part of his army, laying down rules that had to be followed to the letter. Something she hadn't done.

Sir Martin's lip curled disgustedly. 'Neither have you, it seems,' he responded in his clipped military fashion, with a brief glance towards Roarke, which Ginny understood perfectly. He dropped her hand after the merest touch as if it were a live coal. Which it probably was to him.

Ginny was aware that Roarke was looking at her

thoughtfully, but his mother clapped her hands in delight. 'What's this? You have met before?' she beamed, believing she had brought old friends together.

'Miss Harte was once known to my family,' Sir Martin explained tersely.

Ginny smiled mockingly. 'I shall look forward to meeting your son again,' she told him, and knew he wanted to warn her off there and then, but dare not.

'My son is very busy. I don't think he'll have time to meet everyone,' her father declared, being as blunt as he dared.

'And what of your other children?' Ginny went on turning the screw. 'Are they here with you?' As soon as the question left her lips, she knew it was a mistake. She had given him an opening, and she knew he wouldn't fail to take it. All she could do was brace herself.

Contempt flared in Sir Martin's eyes as he went in for the kill. 'I only have one son and one daughter. Surely you remember that?'

Ginny stared him out, but they both knew she had lost ground in their personal battle. 'I had the impression there were more. Never mind. I must reacquaint myself with your wife and daughter, too.'

'I'll be sure to tell them you are here, Miss Harte,' he responded politely, which she knew meant that he would warn them off from seeking her out. 'Now, if you'll excuse me, I think I'd best see what my wife is doing.' With a nod to Marganita and her son, he turned and walked away.

Ginny felt a hard cold knot settle in her stomach as she watched his retreating back. He wouldn't let her see them if he could prevent it, yet he couldn't be watching them all the time. There would be moments when his back was turned, and she would take her chance. Only…what if they didn't want to see her? James had always followed their father's instructions, whilst Lucy had been so young the last time she had seen her. And Mother... Her mother had been worn down years ago. She would take the chance, though, even if it turned out badly.

She sighed and looked away from him to find herself facing Roarke wearing a very serious expression.

'So you've met Sir Martin before?' he said softly, and that gave her nerves a severe jolt. She had been so intent on squaring up to her father, she hadn't considered what Roarke was overhearing. He would have been tantalised, and she knew he was puzzling over the facts, trying to put two and two together.

She shrugged, determined to keep him off the path she knew he wanted to follow. 'It was a long time ago. We didn't get on,' she added and he laughed.

'That was patently obvious, to anyone except my mother. She still believes she's brought two old friends together.'

They had never been friends. 'I preferred his family to him. He isn't an easy man to get along with.'

Roarke glanced off to where Sir Martin had vanished into the crowd. 'He didn't appear to want you to meet his family.'

Ginny let out a hollow laugh. 'There's nothing new in that.'

Roarke's expression went from thoughtful to amused. 'But you're going to do it anyway, aren't you?'

Ginny met his look and started to smile with genuine amusement. 'I never have liked being ordered off,' she confirmed.

'Which makes you a woman after my own heart,' Roarke declared. 'This is turning out to be a far more interesting weekend than I had imagined.'

Interesting wasn't the word she would have chosen, she thought, as she sipped her drink. Dangerous seemed to fit better. Running into her father had been unpleasant, but there was a brighter side. Her family was so close, she could almost touch them. All she had to do was reach out. Life had a way of throwing you a crumb of hope just when you least expected it.

CHAPTER FOUR

DINNER was a sumptuous affair, and Ginny could only wonder what the wedding breakfast would be like. It seemed to her it would be hard to top this. Not that she had a large appetite. Half of the guests had melted away before dinner was announced. They had been invited for cocktails to meet the bride and groom, so it was a smaller number of people sitting around the long table in the formal dining room.

Ginny had caught sight of her mother and sister as they sat down, but they must have received orders not to acknowledge her. Whenever she glanced in their direction they looked away hastily. James had been more subtle. He had simply looked right through her. Not surprising then that her appetite had disappeared.

'Looks like Sir Martin has had a word with his family,' Roarke observed dryly from beside her, and it didn't really surprise Ginny to realise he had seen what was happening. He sensed a mystery, and mysteries had only one reason for existence—to be solved.

'All done with military precision,' she joked.

Roarke reached for his glass of wine and took a sip. 'What did you do to get on the wrong side of him?'

She poked at a piece of chicken with her fork. 'Marching in step was never my forte.'

'If you aren't going to eat that, leave it alone,' Roarke ordered mockingly. 'Didn't your parents tell you not to play with your food?'

Spearing the chicken, she raised it to her mouth with a

challenging look. 'Constantly, but I didn't listen to them,' she declared, and popped the morsel into her mouth. It was dry by now, and she was forced to wash it down with some wine.

'So,' Roarke went on. 'How did you get to meet James Beavis?' he asked curiously.

Ginny toyed with her glass, watching the golden liquid swill from side to side. 'You could say we grew up together,' she admitted wryly.

'I thought he might have been an old flame,' Roarke put in, surprising her into looking at him.

'James?' she exclaimed with a laugh. 'No, there was never anything like that between us.' No doubt he would be angry with her if he ever discovered the true nature of her relationship with James but, as she had no intention of telling him, there was no way he would find out. Her private life was going to remain private.

'Good. I didn't really think he was your type.'

Ginny followed his gaze to where her brother sat talking to Caroline, Roarke's sister. There was nothing animated in his features. Nothing to show he was looking forward to marrying the woman he was talking to. She frowned. She hoped Caroline was doing the right thing. If James had become more like their father... But it was not her decision.

'How on earth did they meet?' she asked, and Roarke shrugged.

'At some charity dinner, so Mother tells me. Perhaps they exchanged horror stories and decided they would be better off together,' he said with a laugh, and Ginny winced.

'Talking of horror stories, your stepmother is unbelievable!' she pronounced in an undertone.

'Oh, yes,' he agreed dryly. 'I liked the way you sat on her. She was no match for you.'

Ginny was pleased he was pleased, but shrugged in an offhand way. 'I was only doing my job.'

'You seemed to be enjoying it,' Roarke pointed out sardonically, and she chuckled.

'OK, so I admit it gave me a certain satisfaction to peel her off you. I didn't like her.'

'The feeling was mutual,' he responded with a laugh.

Ginny laughed too, and as she turned towards him their eyes met in shared enjoyment. Then it seemed to her that something changed, and for a wild moment there was a connection between them. Something other than shared laughter. Her heart lurched, and she saw the tiny frown that appeared between his brows. He started to reach out a hand to her, and she held her breath, waiting...

'Hey, you two, break it up,' one of Roarke's half-brothers called from across the table, and suddenly they were the centre of attention.

Ginny came to with a jolt and felt colour storm into her cheeks. Roarke handled the matter with more *élan*.

'Mind your own business, Tom. Ginny and I are having a private conversation,' he declared, grinning at her. 'Ignore him, darling. He's just jealous because I happen to have the most beautiful woman in the room sitting next to me.'

The endearment took her by surprise, but a second later she realised he was acting a part. His statement was hotly refuted up and down the table and she was able to use the time to gather her composure. Whatever had happened in those odd few seconds, it had been quite unsettling. She didn't know why it had happened, but she would have to take care that nothing like it happened again. Which, she acknowledged wryly, might prove difficult as she hadn't anticipated anything like it happening once.

It was quite late when they left the table and returned to the drawing room. Roarke took her round and introduced her to the other members of his family. They all appeared to be nice, friendly people, who accepted her presence without question, which made her feel something of a fraud, until she reminded herself the deception was in a good cause.

She kept an eye out for her family, but it was an hour or so before she saw James standing on his own for a moment. Knowing there would be few opportunities like this one, she excused herself from the group she was with and made her way towards him. Her brother didn't notice her approach until the very last second, by which time it was impossible for him to escape. He tensed visibly, clearly unhappy with the situation.

A lump of emotion lodged itself in her throat as she smiled at him. 'Hello, James,' she greeted huskily, willing him to respond.

For his part, her brother's eyes darted about the room, and she had no doubt who he was looking for. Not wanting to be interrupted too soon, she placed herself in a position to shield as much of him as she could from the room at large.

'You can speak to me, you know. I won't bite,' she urged softly, trying to tease him as she had been wont to do when they were at home.

Finally he looked at her. 'Go away, Ginny.'

It was hardly encouraging, but she persevered. 'Can't we talk, James? We used to be able to talk, at least.'

James looked angry. 'That was before. Things have changed. I can't talk to you. I won't,' he declared, and made to move away, but her hand on his arm forestalled him.

'Can you still be so afraid of him, James? Even now?' she asked unhappily, and he paled, jerking his arm free.

'I'm tired of hearing that from you. It was so easy for you, Ginny. You had nothing to lose!' he snapped angrily, keeping his voice down with an effort.

Ginny almost laughed as she shook her head. 'You're wrong. I had everything to lose. I lost you and Lucy and Mum. I've missed you. All I want to do is talk to you.'

For the space of a heartbeat James appeared to hesitate, but then something over her shoulder made him shut down tight. She glanced round and saw their father watching them, his expression grim. No wonder James was in retreat.

'Get lost, Ginny!' he snarled at her, and this time he did walk away.

Ginny didn't try to stop him, for she knew there would be no point. James had never been strong enough to fight their father's strictures, even when she had been there to back him up. He hated unpleasantness and rows and angry voices. He had been a gentle boy, which had irritated their father and made him send his son to a military school to toughen him up. James had returned more buttoned-up than ever, and Ginny would never forgive her father for that.

Feeling as she did, she couldn't stay in the same room with him right now, for she didn't know what she might do. She had to get away to calm down. Which was why she didn't return to where Roarke stood talking to another of his sisters, but headed for the terrace and the fresh air. Nor was she aware that he watched her go, a frown of concern creasing his forehead.

Outside, she headed away from the light cast by the doorway, into the peace of the shadows further along where few people had wandered to. Resting her hands on the parapet, she tipped her head back, allowing the breeze that blew in off the lake to cool her face. It lifted the hair from her neck and she rolled her head slowly from side to side to get maximum benefit. It felt wonderful, and she could feel herself relaxing.

She might not have felt so relaxed had she been aware of the man who had followed her out and who now approached her from behind. She had only the briefest of warnings given by the sound of a footfall, then Sir Martin's hand took her by the shoulder and spun her round roughly.

His face was livid with anger. 'My God, why must you constantly defy me? I told you to stay away from my son. We want nothing to do with you.'

Ginny had never been afraid of confrontation, no matter how threatening her father could be. Now she rested back against the stonework of the low wall and tipped her chin up at him.

'You disowned me, remember? Which means you no longer have the right to tell me what I may or may not do,' she shot right back, unaware of a dark figure who slipped out of a window further along the veranda and settled into the shadows. 'I'm no longer your daughter, Brigadier.'

Sir Martin's lip curled scornfully. 'You were never that. A daughter doesn't disobey her father. She doesn't mix with riff-raff, nor sleep with gutter trash! A daughter thinks more of herself than to bed down with any man who asks her!'

Ginny could feel the same old anger balling up inside her, threatening to choke her. 'My friends were not riff-raff,' she insisted, enunciating each word carefully. 'Nor did I ever sleep around.'

He laughed harshly. 'No? You went off with the first man who came sniffing round you. You couldn't wait to get into his bed!'

The accusation was true, but only to a point. 'I loved him. I thought he loved me.' She had been desperate for affection, starving for it. So much so that she was blinded to Mark's true nature.

That made Sir Martin laugh again. 'And all he really wanted was *my* money. When he knew he would never get his hands on it, he couldn't drop you quickly enough.'

Ginny crossed her arms over her chest to hide the fact that her hands were shaking with suppressed emotion. 'I wasn't the first, and I certainly won't be the last woman who's been made a fool of by a man.'

'Nor been left pregnant by him,' Sir Martin added sneeringly.

There was nothing Ginny could do to ward off the shaft of pain his words drove through her. She gasped as the old wound was torn open. Straightening up, her eyes flashed a warning he was treading on dangerous ground.

'That has nothing to do with you.'

Her father bent over her, using his height and size to dominate. 'It has everything to do with me, young woman. I have to live with the knowledge that there's a fatherless child out there bringing disgrace to an old and honoured name!'

Oh, if ever there were a few words that summed up what really mattered to her father, those were the ones. His name and position meant more to him than his family. Well, he didn't have to worry about it any longer.

Strong emotions threatened to choke her, but she forced herself to speak clearly. 'You can put your mind at rest, Brigadier. There is no child to put a blot on the family escutcheon.'

He was brought up short temporarily. 'You had it adopted after all?'

That was what he had demanded in exchange for his help. It had never been an option for her. Ginny shook her head. 'She died.' Her voice broke on the word, and her eyes glittered like diamonds with unshed tears. 'That should give you cause to celebrate,' she went on, rallying. Determined not to break down before this unforgiving man.

Sir Martin straightened up, folding his hands behind his back, military fashion. 'Probably the best thing to happen,' he declared shortly, and Ginny drew in a shocked breath.

'You are incredible. There isn't an ounce of compassion in you. Well, this will come as a surprise to you, Brigadier, but it wasn't the best thing for me that my baby died. I wanted her. I would have loved her in a way you could never comprehend.'

Sir Martin set his jaw. 'Children are for continuing the family line.'

How many times had she heard that? It had been no more true then than it was now. 'That's archaic! You would have had me marry a man of your choice, just to enhance the family connection!'

'Precisely. James and Lucy are doing their duty by the family, as you should have done.'

Ginny paled at his revelation. 'You're forcing Lucy into marriage, too?'

'Nobody is forcing her to do anything. I've simply placed the names of suitable husbands before her so that she can make her own choice,' her father denied.

'And if she doesn't want to marry one of those?' Ginny enquired, feeling her stomach tighten as Sir Martin smiled smugly.

'Lucy is not like you. She will do what she knows is right, or end up like you.'

Ginny stared at him, aghast. 'You're using me as a threat to get her to do what you demand?' Her brain was whirling. Oh, God, Lucy, not you too!

Sir Martin smirked down at her. 'Did you think you would be sowing the seeds of rebellion when you left? That was a serious tactical error. All you did was remove a thorn in my side. Your name is never mentioned. You don't exist so far as this family is concerned, Virginia. My game, I think.'

Ginny closed her eyes as she made a sickening discovery. By staying away she had given her father the opportunity to force her brother and sister into line. Too late she realised she should have stayed in touch with them somehow. She could have helped them to see that they didn't have to obey his unreasonable demands. As he said, it had been a tactical error on her part, but he had just made one of his own. He had told her about it, and now she knew she had to do something. James might be beyond her reach, but Lucy was not. What she must not do now was show her hand.

'You may think you've won, Brigadier, but it's an illusion. You're going to end up a lonely, bitter old man. Now, if you don't mind, I came out here for some fresh air, and you're sullying it with your presence.'

'I have no intention of staying out here any longer than it takes me to get your promise not to talk to my family,' Sir Martin responded coldly, but Ginny laughed and shook her head.

'Hell will freeze over before that happens.'

Angry colour mottled his cheeks. 'You refuse?'

'You can bet your life I do. You can't browbeat me

like you do James. I'm made of stronger stuff.' Hopefully, Lucy would be made of stronger stuff too. Lord, she hoped so.

He looked as if he wanted to throttle her, but that was one thing he had never done—harmed any of them physically. He preferred to dominate mentally. 'You'll regret defying me. I'll make sure you do,' he threatened, and spun on his heel and marched off.

Shaking more than a little, Ginny turned and rested her hands on the parapet again, closing her eyes.

'Damn him! Oh, damn him to hell!' she gritted out through her teeth, slamming her fist on to the concrete.

Her father had dominated her life, turned it into an unending war for independence. She had thought she was free, but it had been a temporary reprieve. She would not be able to breathe freely again until she had saved Lucy from a marriage of convenience. Lucy had been scarcely ten years old when she had left—a child—now she was a young woman. Perhaps it was too late. Her father might have done his work too well. It was something Ginny was going to have to find out...

Suddenly she froze. There had been a noise off to her left followed by a stifled sound. Turning round, she tried to probe the darkness.

'Hello? Is anybody there?' she called out, and was almost on the point of deciding it must have been a cat or some other animal, when the darkness shifted and she could make out the shape of a man walking towards her.

Seconds later, Roarke stepped into the soft moonlight, a wry expression on his face. 'I should tell my mother to move some of her potted plants. I gave my knee a nasty rap,' he said with a laugh, but Ginny didn't smile.

'What were you doing, hovering in the shadows like

that?' she demanded to know, whilst a cold lump settled in her stomach. How long had he been there? What did he know?

'Enjoying the moonlight?' Roarke ventured, but when she continued to stare at him coldly, he shrugged and confessed. 'Waiting for Sir Martin to leave.'

Her eyes narrowed. 'How long have you been standing there?'

Roarke came closer, hands tucked into his trouser pockets. 'I saw him follow you out, and, as I didn't like the look on his face, I decided to keep tabs on him. I slipped out through the library window.' He jerked his head in the direction of the window she could barely make out.

Her nerves jolted anxiously at that, and though she was sure she knew the answer to her next question, she braced herself to ask it anyway. 'How much did you hear?'

Stopping before her, Roarke looked her squarely in the eye. 'Pretty much everything,' he confessed, and Ginny drew in an angry breath. By her sides her hands balled into fists.

'Damn you, Roarke, you had no right to listen! What you eavesdropped on was private.'

He raised his hands placatingly. 'I know. I'm sorry. In my defence, I can only say I was more interested in making sure you were safe. I told you, I didn't like the look on your father's face.'

The casual use of the word 'father' underlined just how much he now knew, and how pointless it would be to attempt to deny it. The cat was out of the bag and, much as she might wish otherwise, it could never be put back. Roarke now knew the most sordid details of her past, and she was sure he could make a good attempt at filling in the blanks of what he didn't know. The protective wall she had built had been breached, leaving her feeling more exposed and vulnerable than she had in years. Impotent rage bubbled inside her, and she hated him for knowing what he did. It was none of his business.

'What you did was despicable, and a sheer waste of time.' She hit back at him the only way she could. 'I was never in any physical danger from him. That isn't how he works.'

Roarke's expression grew grim. 'No, I realised that after a while. He prefers to use mind games, doesn't he? Where the scars won't show. It's still abuse in my book. Your father is little more than a bully, and I have an intense dislike for bullies.'

Ginny folded her arms and paced up and down. 'Maybe you do, but that didn't give you the right to follow us. Besides, I can take care of myself,' she insisted, ending up before him and glaring at him frostily.

Roarke smiled, but it was far from pleasant. 'I'm glad to hear it, but if I hear him threatening you again I'll knock him into the middle of next week, and I won't ask your permission first.'

The statement so surprised her that Ginny blinked at him. 'You'll what?'

Roarke continued to look grimly purposeful. 'You heard me.'

Nobody had ever come to her defence before. Ginny had always fought a lonely battle, for herself and her brother and sister, and to have someone say what he just had drained her anger and left her more than a little bemused. She sat down a tad hurriedly on the parapet.

'But I'm not your responsibility, Roarke,' she felt compelled to remind him, to which he shot her a level look.

'You're my responsibility if I choose to make you so…and I do choose to make you so.'

That caused her to laugh mockingly. 'Oh, yeah? You don't even like me!'

Roarke shrugged. 'You're growing on me,' he admitted, and moved round to rest against the wall beside her. 'So that's your family, huh?'

She pulled a face. 'Not any more. You heard the Brigadier say so himself.' It felt strange to be talking openly about them after all these years. Because it had hurt so much to be cut off from them, it had been easier not to talk about them at all. By overhearing what he had, Roarke had just broken down that barrier too. Though she hated that he knew, he was one person she had no need to lie to now. Surprisingly, that gave her a new-found sense of freedom.

Roarke glanced at her sideways. 'Why do you call him Brigadier?'

'Because he was never a father. He issued orders, or gave us rules and regulations which had to be followed to the letter and, if we didn't, privileges were withdrawn. Our friends had to be vetted before they were allowed in the house. We were his family, but he treated us as if we were part of the army.'

'Charming man,' Roarke remarked scathingly. 'I'm not surprised you rebelled. I'm just surprised you stayed so long.'

'It wasn't through lack of nerve,' she hastily justified herself. 'If I had run away they would only have brought me back home, and that would have been worse. So I decided to wait it out until I was old enough to leave. It was while I was waiting that I met Mark the Snake,' she added, keeping her tone level with an effort.

'There are a lot of those around,' Roarke pronounced wryly. 'It isn't always easy to pick the good guys from the bad guys, sweetheart. For one thing, the bad guys have good camouflage.'

Ginny shot him a whimsical look. 'Where were you when I needed some good advice?' she asked sardonically, and he chuckled.

'Creating my own kind of hell, probably. Do I take it your romance with Mark the Snake followed the usual pattern?'

Ginny had never thought she would find anything amusing about the past, but Roarke's comments made her smile and eased the remembered sense of despair. 'You do. I thought he loved me, but the Brigadier was quite right. All he wanted was the money that would come with me. When I was cut off he vanished quicker than you can say it.' Leaving her pregnant and without the means to support herself, but she wasn't ready to talk about that to Roarke yet.

'Snakes have a habit of doing that. You were better off without him in the long run,' Roarke observed evenly, and Ginny nodded.

'True, but I was still living short term. There were... complications.' She had struggled on, but it had been a downward path which had eventually sent her back to her family, only to be rejected because she wouldn't give up her baby. She shivered at the memory and took a slightly ragged breath. 'It was the worst time of my life and I prefer not to think about it.'

Roarke nodded. 'I can understand that. You have to move on.'

His understanding was unexpected but welcome. 'I made another life for myself and I thought I'd left the past behind.'

'Until you discovered your brother is marrying my sister,' he mused thoughtfully.

'Seeing the Brigadier again after all these years was a nasty shock. I couldn't think why he would be here,' Ginny confirmed.

'I can't say I like the sound of the family Caroline's marrying into.'

Ginny could well understand his concern. He cared about his family, and wouldn't want his sister to walk into the lion's den. She glanced down at her fingers, knowing it was within her means to put his mind at rest. It would mean revealing more of herself to a stranger, but the thought of doing nothing didn't sit easily with her.

'Listen, I can talk to her if you like. Tell her what my father can be like. She's in no danger, though. After all, she's the good connection the Brigadier wants for his son. If she produces an heir in nine months' time, she'll be his pride and joy.'

Roarke glanced at her downbent head. 'A legitimate heir,' he said gently, and Ginny stiffened at the reminder. Her eyes darted to his, saw the ready sympathy there, and rejected it. He was going too far. She jumped to her feet, crossing her arms and taking a hasty step away.

'Don't even think of going there, Roarke. You overheard things that were none of your business. The subject isn't open for discussion,' she told him forthrightly, her eyes sending sparks his way as she looked at him.

'I merely wanted to say I'm sorry about your baby.'

Ginny fashioned a shrug of sorts, although her heart twisted painfully. 'It was a long time ago.'

Roarke shook his head. 'Sweetheart, it was only yesterday for you, and always will be,' he countered gently, bringing a lump to her throat and tears to her eyes.

She held up a hand to silence him. 'So help me, Roarke, if you say another word…' Her throat closed over at that point, and she turned her face away, closing her eyes, pressing her lips together tightly to still their trembling.

She didn't hear him rise and come up behind her, just the gentle touch of his hands on her shoulders.

'Forgive me. I'm not usually so crass,' he apologised and his thumbs took up a sensuous circling motion.

'You weren't crass. You were trying to be kind, and I thank you for that, but I'd rather just forget this whole episode.'

Ginny knew she ought to shrug him away, but his touch was giving off an incredible amount of warmth that was sending tingles through her bloodstream. It had the strange effect of making her want to lean back against him. It was very tempting, hypnotically so, and she might even have done it if a couple hadn't walked out of the open door, laughing at something someone had said. She was brought back to the present with a jolt.

'Hey! Cut that out!' she ordered immediately.

Stepping away from him, so that his hands fell to his sides, she asked herself just what she thought she was doing letting him touch her at all, let alone leaning in to him! He was the man she loved to hate, though she had to admit there were aspects of him which weren't as bad as she had thought. Her heightened emotions were no doubt playing tricks on her after the encounter with her father.

Roarke held up his hands and backed off. 'Sorry. I thought you liked it.'

She had, but that was hardly the point. 'Look, I know you were trying to help, but keep your hands to yourself in future.'

He winced and glanced towards the couple who were strolling towards them. 'OK, OK, just keep your voice down. We're supposed to be an item, remember?'

How could she forget? 'We'd better go in,' she suggested.

'Are you still willing to talk to my sister?'

'Of course.' Ginny wasn't about to withdraw her offer. Caroline needed to know what she was taking on.

'Let's go find her, then.' He led the way to the door, but halted short of entering the crowded room. 'Wait a second.'

Ginny halted obediently. 'What's wrong?'

He grinned wolfishly. 'Nothing—just checking you look as if we've been up to something.'

Ginny shot him a withering look. 'Well, do I?'

'Don't worry—only you, me and Sir Martin know what really went on. To the rest you look interestingly mussed.'

'Oh, good!'

Taking her arm, he slipped it through his and laughed huskily. 'Behave yourself, we're about to walk out on stage again.'

Ginny rolled her eyes, then plastered a smile to her lips. 'If I wish you to break a leg, you won't misunderstand my meaning, will you?' she hissed out of the side of her mouth.

'Ouch!' Roarke laughed again and they stepped inside.

CHAPTER FIVE

UNFORTUNATELY Ginny and Roarke didn't get the chance to talk to Caroline before the party wound down. They mingled and waited and watched, but James stayed firmly by his fiancée's side, making it impossible for them to speak to her freely.

'We'll catch up with her later, after the others have gone to bed,' Roarke decided as the clock slowly ticked towards midnight.

'What if James is with her?' Ginny pointed out, but Roarke shook his head.

'In this house? Not a chance.'

Her brows rose. 'We're together.'

He grinned roguishly. 'That's because I'm a hopeless case, and we aren't getting married tomorrow, or is it today? Now, if we should find my mother with her, offering her some last-minute unwanted advice, that wouldn't surprise me at all.'

Ginny had been carrying an untouched glass of wine around with her for ages, and now set it down on the nearest table. 'This is getting ridiculous. I'm tired. Let's go to bed,' she grumbled, stifling a yawn.

'Now, that's the best offer I've had all day,' Roarke flirted wickedly.

'It wasn't an offer,' she refuted immediately, knowing that, had she been less tired, she would have chosen her words more carefully. 'It was a statement. I'm tired,' she repeated grumpily. It had been a long day, and unexpectedly emotional. She was drained.

'You're no fun, sweetheart,' Roarke teased. 'You were supposed to get affronted and flash those fascinating eyes at me,' he added, causing her to frown.

'I'm too tired to get affronted. And what do you mean, fascinating eyes?' she asked in surprise.

He laughed softly. 'When I've made you really mad at me, you spear me with a look.'

'I do not,' she protested, still unexpectedly unsettled by his description of her eyes.

'Sure you do. Lesser men would tremble, but I'm made of sterner stuff. I can take it.'

'Which is just as well, because you probably deserve it,' she riposted smartly, then a movement across the room caught her eye. 'Oh, look, I think your sister may be calling it a night.'

Roarke glanced round in time to see Caroline kiss her mother and say a general goodnight to whoever was left in the room before leaving with James.

'We'll give them ten minutes to say goodnight to each other, then we'll follow her. Can you last out till then?'

Ginny nodded. Another half an hour wasn't going to make a lot of difference. 'If we go outside, the air should wake me up a bit,' she suggested.

'Come on, then. We'll stroll round the house and go up by the back stairs.'

The cooling midnight air did clear her head as they slowly strolled along the terrace. At the corner they halted by mutual consent to study the view over the lake. It was such a clear night, with the lights of the town glittering almost as much as the stars overhead.

'It really is beautiful here,' Ginny observed with an envious sigh.

'I try to come over several times during the summer,' Roarke agreed.

She quirked an eyebrow at him, lips twitching impishly. 'To visit the ogre? Isn't that taking filial duty a little too far?'

His laugh was rueful. 'You're never going to let me forget that, are you?' he said, reaching out to brush a strand of red hair from her cheek.

'Hey!' Ginny protested without any great force. 'We're not on stage now,' she reminded him. Much to her surprise, he didn't remove his hand but brushed an imaginary strand from her other cheek.

'As a matter of fact, we are,' he countered softly, and her eyes widened. 'We're being watched.'

She went still. 'Who is it?'

'My over-sexed stepmother. She must have seen us come out here and decided to follow to see what we get up to,' Roarke enlarged and met her eyes. 'She knows I wouldn't miss an opportunity like this for a little romancing. We're going to have to give her a show, I'm afraid, or she'll start to smell a rat.'

Ginny desperately wanted to look round, but that would have been too obvious. All she could do was hold his gaze. 'What do you mean? Exactly what kind of show?'

With a casual movement Roarke stepped in front of her and set his hands on her shoulders. 'Brace yourself, sweetheart. I'm going to have to kiss you. Nothing else will do.'

He began to lower his head towards hers, and Ginny raised her hands to his chest. 'I didn't agree to any of this hands-on stuff.'

Roarke's lips twitched. 'What did they used to say: close your eyes and think of England? Don't worry, it will all be over in a minute,' he joked, and brought his mouth down on hers.

And that was how it began.

The kiss started out as a simple pressing of lips on lips, and probably would have stayed that way, only something happened that changed everything. Ginny was thinking she would give him 'think of England'…when her brain stopped functioning. She was unexpectedly swamped by a powerful wave of electricity which lit her up from inside and set her nerve-ends tingling. Heat surged through her system, bringing with it a sensual response that had her lips softening and parting. Before she knew it one kiss became two, then many as they sought more of the same, tasting and exploring with ever-deepening need. They couldn't seem to get enough.

Without conscious thought she let her hands slip up around his neck, her fingers fastening in his hair, whilst at the same time Roarke let out a purely male groan and slid his arms around her, pulling her tight up against himself. When Roarke's tongue sought her mouth Ginny welcomed him with a sigh of pleasure, matching him stroke for stroke. They drowned in the kiss, and at the same time it began to spiral out of control. Neither seemed able, or willing, to stop it.

The angry banging of a door echoed across the night and startled them back to the present. The kiss ended, leaving them staring at each other in slowly dawning realisation that they were in each other's arms and couldn't remember how they had got there. Of course, that situation didn't last. They simultaneously recalled that the kiss was supposed to be no more than a gesture, and their shock was mirrored on both faces.

'Oh, my God!' Ginny declared thickly, very much aware that her heart was racing, her knees were trembling and her breathing was ragged.

'What the hell—?' Roarke muttered unevenly, and released her just as she stepped back from him.

They stared at each other in disbelief. Roarke raised a faintly trembling hand and dragged it through his hair.

'Well, that was unexpected!' he attempted to joke, but the words came out heartfelt. He meant what he said and it was no laughing matter—for either of them.

Ginny touched a finger to lips that felt slightly swollen. 'Tell me that didn't happen,' she commanded in horror.

Roarke laughed hollowly. 'What did just happen?' he wanted to know, but Ginny couldn't help him.

Of course, they both knew what had happened, but neither wanted to believe it. The kiss was supposed to have been a token gesture. It had turned into a passionate conflagration that still had their bodies tingling.

Ginny turned away from him, striving to get her breathing back to normal. 'This isn't happening. I don't want this.'

'You think I do?' Roarke growled behind her.

Ginny licked her lips, but that was a mistake, for she could still taste him. 'Just...don't start getting any wild ideas, OK.'

'Sweetheart, I don't want to have any ideas about you!'

She spun round again, eyes flashing accusingly. 'Then why did you kiss me like that?'

'Why did you?' Roarke countered, and they were left staring at each other in angry silence.

It was Ginny who finally broke the hiatus. 'This is a silly thing to be arguing over. Neither of us planned it, it just happened. It must have been moon madness. Things like this often happen at weddings, but it doesn't mean anything. It isn't going to happen again.'

'You can say that again,' Roarke agreed dryly. 'Hopefully, Jenna will have got the message.'

Their eyes met, and both knew the other was thinking that the message she had got was more than either had bargained for. Then it hit them that they hadn't given Jenna a thought, and they turned as one to find the terrace empty.

'She's gone,' Roarke confirmed. 'It must have been the door closing that…' He left the sentence hanging for Ginny to fill in the blanks.

'Yes, well, I think we should draw a veil over the last ten minutes and call it a night,' Ginny suggested uncomfortably.

'We still have to see my sister,' he reminded her.

'It's getting late, Roarke. She could be asleep already. We can see her first thing in the morning. Your mother isn't going to let James anywhere near her before the wedding, so the coast will be clear,' Ginny pointed out, wishing she had thought of that earlier, then that kiss—or kisses—need never have happened.

'You're right,' Roarke agreed, clearly in no mood to prolong the evening either. 'Tomorrow will be better.'

By which time she should have got her head round what had happened tonight, and put it in perspective. It was laughable to think that she and Roarke could be attracted to each other. It had been a momentary aberration, and the clear light of day would put their relationship back on its customary footing. She had no doubt of that…no doubt at all.

Back in their bedroom, they barely spoke. Ginny collected her night things and disappeared into the bathroom. When she came out again, Roarke had taken a pillow and cover from the bed and made up the couch. Without a word, he went into the bathroom whilst Ginny hung up her things in the dressing room and hurried into bed. She had turned out the light and closed her eyes when Roarke reappeared. She heard him move about carefully in the darkness, then all noises ceased.

It wasn't easy to sleep, and she tossed and turned for some time before her exhausted body gave up the struggle and she slept. Roarke tucked his hand under the pillow and studied the moonlight on the ceiling. On the bedside table her travel clock slowly ticked on.

Ginny was dreaming. It was a dream she hadn't had for a long time, but it was no less powerful for all that. It was not a pleasant dream, but good dreams rarely returned to haunt a person. She was caught in the past, trapped by memories that came thick and fast. Unable to break free, she tossed and turned restlessly.

The nightmare was always the same. It was night, but she dared not put the light on, for the landlord of the grotty bedsit she called home was due to call to collect the rent and she didn't have the money. She had a job washing dishes—it paid little, but it was all she could get. She had been sick all through her pregnancy, and it had lost her the few better paid jobs she had managed to get. Now her boss had threatened to fire her if she was late again—and she was late already...

The scene changed. Now she was standing outside the cheap restaurant, with the manager telling her to clear off. She tried to plead with him, but he didn't want to know. She had to turn, had to take the next step. Anxiety began to rise in her, and her head thrashed about on the pillow. She didn't want to go on, but the dream was remorseless. It took her back down that dingy street as she made her way home. As always, she didn't hear the approach of the person who jumped her, just felt a shove in the back and hands grabbing for her bag. Beneath the covers her legs and arms thrashed about as, in her dream, she fought him, hanging on to the bag, for it contained all the money she had. But her pregnancy had made her clumsy and weak, and with one last shove he had got the bag and run.

She cried out, but it didn't wake her, and for the hundredth time she careered into the heavy-duty bins and fell to the floor of the alleyway. And, as night followed day, there came the pains, making her groan in her sleep. In her dream she called for help, but nobody came, and she lay there in the dark, in pain, knowing her baby was coming and that she had to try to help herself. Tears streamed down her face as somehow she managed to get to her knees and crawl out to the road. Then more pain and she collapsed, and she knew she was going to lose her baby…

Dragged from an uneasy sleep, Roarke lay on the couch and tried to get his bearings. Then he heard sounds from across the room and sat up, glancing to the bed Ginny occupied. He could just make out the thrashing movements beneath the covers, and it was closely followed by a sound that turned his blood cold. Ginny was crying. Painful sobs that tore into the very heart of him and brought him to his feet in a hurry.

Padding to the bed, he stared down at her, knowing she wouldn't want him anywhere near her, but knowing too that he couldn't leave her trapped in the midst of the despairing dream she was having. Easing himself on to the edge of the bed, he reached out to gently shake her awake.

'Wake up, Ginny. Ginny, can you hear me? It's a dream. Come on, sweetheart, snap out of it!'

Ginny heard a voice calling her from a long way away. An insistent voice that dragged her out of the depths of her nightmare, leaving the pain behind but not the sense of loss. She felt hands lifting her, shaking her, and with a ragged gasp she woke.

She blinked at the figure who sat on the bed, holding her by the shoulders. 'Roarke?'

'You were crying in your sleep. Must have been a very bad dream.' He explained his presence, eyes quartering her face in concern.

Ginny touched her hand to her cheeks and they came away moist. 'Oh, God!' she whispered achingly. She knew what dream it had been; the tendrils of it came drifting back, coiling around her heart, making her shiver in remembrance. 'Did I wake you? I'm sorry. I should have known...'

Releasing her now that she was awake, Roarke sat back. 'Known what? That seeing your father again would bring the memories back?'

She nodded, not really surprised by his astuteness. 'I haven't had that one in a while.' She had been hoping she would never have it again, but she should have known better.

'Was it about your father?'

Ginny rubbed her hands over her arms, warding off a chill that came more from inside than out. 'Not really.'

Indirectly, her father's refusal to help her had set her along a path which had ultimately led to the loss of her baby, but she wouldn't put the blood on his hands.

'Do you want to talk about it?' Roarke offered. 'I've been told I'm a very good listener.'

Ginny shook her head in swift refusal. 'No. I don't even want to think about it.'

He accepted that without argument. 'Can I get you anything? Hot milk? Chocolate?'

'I'll be fine,' Ginny declared confidently, though she knew from experience that she wouldn't be. Whenever she had had the dream before, sleeping afterwards had been impossible. But she wasn't his problem. She would deal with it. She had always dealt with it.

'OK, but you know where I am if you need me,' he told her as he got off the bed.

Ginny lay back against her pillows and listened to the sound of Roarke returning to his bed on the couch. She tried to keep her breathing light and did her best not to move about too much, wanting him to go back to sleep. Time passed slowly, but eventually she was sure he must no longer be awake, so she sat up, plumping the pillows behind her and stared out of the window, watching for a sign that would tell her dawn was approaching.

'What's the matter, Ginny?'

The disembodied voice drifting to her from the couch made her jump. 'I thought you were asleep.'

'I was waiting for you to drop off. At this rate, it looks as if neither of us will get any more sleep tonight,' he remarked without rancour.

The last thing she wanted to do was disturb anyone other than herself. 'Don't let me keep you awake,' she urged him, but should have known better by now.

'Ginny, you can't expect me to turn over and start knocking out zeds when I know darn well you're afraid to sleep.'

Her heart leapt into her throat at his intuition. 'I'm not...' she began, but the rest of the sentence trailed off, because it was a lie and they both knew it. 'You're right, I am scared. I know from experience that if I sleep now I'll only have the dream again. Once is enough for any night,' she added with a shudder.

'What's it about, this dream?'

Ginny pulled her legs up and wrapped her arms around them protectively. 'The worst day of my life,' she admitted scratchily.

'I guess that would have to be the time you lost your baby,' Roarke stated softly, not wanting her to draw back into her shell.

She was getting used to him pulling rabbits out of the hat this way. 'You guessed correctly.'

'Have you ever spoken to anyone about that time?' Roarke probed carefully.

Ginny shook her head, then, realising he couldn't see the gesture, cleared her throat. 'No.' Who had there been to talk to? Her family had been denied her, and her old friends had drifted away into their own lives.

'Talking helps, Ginny. Keeping it locked up inside yourself is asking for bad dreams to come.'

She knew he was right. The past was festering inside her, never healing. She had to get it out in the open for her own sake. He wasn't the person she would have chosen to talk to, but he knew so much already there seemed little point in hiding the rest.

'How good a listener are you?' she asked wryly.

'The best. I don't judge, and I don't tell tales. Try me.'

Ginny sighed heavily. 'Where do I begin? My life had become such a mess by then. The start of it all was when I left with Mark. Nothing went right from then on.'

'Except the baby,' Roarke corrected evenly, and she smiled faintly.

'You're right. Except the baby. I wanted her. I was prepared to move mountains to give her what I had missed.' Her smile faded away. 'The day I discovered I was pregnant was the day Mark left me. He never knew about the baby. My father had cut me off, and Mark saw his meal ticket slipping out of his grasp. I didn't know at the time, but he had gone to see the Brigadier, to try and get him to change his mind. I could have told him it wouldn't work. He said no, and a week later Mark disappeared. Whilst I was waiting for hours for him to come home so I could tell him about the baby, he was miles away cutting his losses.'

Roarke made himself comfortable with his hands behind his head, listening to the flat voice tell its tale. 'You never saw him again?'

'I had no idea where to look. He told me very little about himself. Besides, when the bills that he had run up started to come in, I fell out of love very quickly. It wasn't hard to decide to bring up my baby on my own, but from the start things were against me. I had an awful pregnancy. The sickness they told me would eventually stop, never did. I lost I don't know how many jobs because the sickness prevented me from working. Money became tight.'

'So you went to your father?'

Ginny closed her eyes against painful memories. 'He wouldn't let me in the house, even when I told him about the baby. He said things…'

Roarke's face grew tight. 'I've heard him. I can guess what he said.'

Ginny dropped her head to her knees. 'He said I could come back, so long as it was without the baby. I refused, and he shut the door in my face.'

'The man wants taking out and shooting!'

'Amen to that.'

Roarke let a little time pass before pressing on. 'What happened then?'

On the bed, Ginny shrugged, keeping her voice level, trying not to feel anything as she told the sorry story. 'I went back to my grotty bedsit and did the best I could. Things got worse, though, and by the time I was seven months' pregnant I owed back rent and was down to washing dishes. That last day I was sick again, and I had this ache low down in my back all day. When the landlord came for the rent, I hid in the dark. I had to wait ages for him to go and that made me late for work. I lost my job.

'I thought that was the darkest moment, but I was wrong. As I walked home, wondering what I was going to do now, someone snatched my bag. I fought them, because I couldn't afford to lose the money in it, but they were stronger than I was and shoved me into an alley.' She felt again those hard hands pushing her. 'There were several large metal bins in there and I must have hit one of them, because I ended up on the floor.' Ginny felt her pulse pick up, and she licked her lips to moisten them. 'That was when the pain started.'

'Go on,' Roarke urged her, even as his own stomach twisted into a knot at what he knew was coming.

'I managed to crawl out of the alley, but that was all. Someone must have found me, because the next thing I can remember I was in an ambulance. Then everything begins to blur. I remember patches. People bending over me. Lights. The smell of disinfectant. Voices telling me to do this or that.' She swallowed hard as memories came rushing back, but the lump remained in her throat. 'Do you know what sound echoes the loudest in my mind? Her cry when she was born. It was so weak, barely there, and I knew then that something was wrong.' Tears welled up in her eyes, and her lips trembled. 'In my heart I knew I wasn't going to have her for long.'

A teardrop overflowed, and then another. She felt the bed depress, and only then realised that Roarke had left the couch. She stared at him, her eyes filled with an unutterable sadness. 'She lived for six hours. I held her hand. It was so tiny, Roarke. She seemed to hold on to me for a while…and then she died. My beautiful baby daughter died,' she whispered achingly, and the tears that she had held back all these years finally found release.

She didn't feel Roarke take her in his arms and rock her whilst the tears fell and she gave vent to her despair in long raking sobs. She cried until her throat ached and there were no more tears to shed. She wept for a life that had been cut tragically short, and for the love she had been unable to give. Finally she was still, and she sighed raggedly.

'I loved her,' she said huskily.

'Only a fool would doubt it,' Roarke returned gently, stroking a soothing hand down her back.

It was that which made Ginny aware of where she was, cradled against the warmth of his strong male chest. She could have felt awkward, but she didn't. For the first time in for ever she felt…comforted. It was a strange sensation, considering who it was who held her.

'I never meant to cry all over you,' she apologised a little awkwardly.

'Something tells me those tears have been a long time coming,' he observed, looking down at her, and Ginny sighed.

'I couldn't cry, because I knew that if I started I would never stop, the pain was so bad. Instead I put all my energy into making something of my life. I got a job, took evening classes. Found a better job, and so on.'

Driving her on had been the need to stay one step ahead of her grief. Allied to a determination to never allow her emotions to blind her. Passion was a drug that scrambled the mind, leaving her open to hurt and betrayal. But she had learned her lesson and passion was out. This time she was going to be in control of her life. This time…

A yawn took her by surprise.

'Think you can sleep now?' Roarke queried.

'Um-hum,' she mumbled. Her eyelids felt weighted, and she decided to shut them for just a few seconds, then she would send him back to the couch.

Roarke listened to the measured sound of her breathing and smiled wryly. She was already asleep but he didn't want to disturb her, so he would wait a few minutes before settling her back on the bed. Making himself comfortable against the pillows, he hooked her in more securely and closed his eyes.

CHAPTER SIX

GINNY drifted to consciousness feeling warm and cosy. Sighing, she rubbed her cheek against the pillow—and something tickled her nose. She moved her hand to brush it away, and her fingers encountered more of the tickly material. Puzzled, she opened her eyes and discovered her 'pillow' was a man's chest, and the 'tickly material' the silky hairs that grew there. Furthermore, her 'pillow' was rising and falling rhythmically as it breathed.

Lifting her head carefully, she could see a stubbly jaw and ruffled black hair and recognised both as belonging to Roarke. Her eyes widened in surprise, and then the memories slowly returned. Last night she had had that dream again. Roarke had heard her, and he had urged her to talk about it. She had, and she had cried too. Cried tears that had been battened down inside her too long. The crying had drained her, and she must have fallen asleep in his arms, but why was she still there? Why hadn't he gone back to the couch? Because he had fallen asleep too, came the obvious answer.

Ginny bit her lip and glanced down at the body she was literally draped around. She had certainly made herself comfortable, she thought dryly. He had some body, though, was the thought that swiftly followed. She had been right; there wasn't an ounce of spare flesh on him. Her eyes began a lazy perusal of long legs and strong thighs, skipped over loins hidden by his shorts, and roved on over a flat stomach, that powerful chest and broad shoulders. Tanned and healthy and pretty much perfect, she decided whimsically.

She wondered what all that bronzed skin felt like to the touch. Her pulse-rate increased slightly as she considered the prospect of running her hand over his chest. A tiny voice in the back of her mind asked her what she thought she was doing, but with the thought had come a need to touch him, to know, and the voice was quashed.

Ginny set her hand down gently and held her breath as she moved it through the forest of silky hair. His skin was smooth, and touching it sent a tingle up her arm that slowly spread through her whole system. Her senses sprang to life, and she could feel her heart racing. That tiny voice urged her to stop, to be sensible, but she was enthralled by the sensations she was experiencing.

So caught up was she that it took a while for her to register that his chest was no longer rising and falling gently but much more powerfully as he dragged in air. Shock at the knowledge that Roarke was awake brought her head up, startled green eyes locking with smouldering grey ones. Time seemed to stand still, but then those eyes dropped to her lips, and they tingled as if he had actually touched them. She couldn't help but moisten her lips with the tip of her tongue. With a growl Roarke's fingers tangled in her fiery hair and eased her up those few inches necessary to allow his mouth to take hers.

It was no gentle kiss, but a sensuous invasion that sought pleasure even as it gave it. The intensity was mind-blowing, for it seemed as if they were intent on devouring each other. Ginny could feel her body responding to the stimulation and, as she moved against him instinctively, she felt the powerful response of his body too. Her stomach clenched, and that familiar ache started deep within her. She wanted him…badly.

'Roarke…' His name was a low moan in her throat as he tore his mouth from hers only to plunder the sensitive cord of her neck. She felt dizzy. Caught up in an over-whelming maelstrom of sensations. Her heart was tapping out a crazy beat…

But it wasn't her heart she could hear. Penetrating through the passion-induced mists in her brain, she slowly realised that what she could hear was a frantic tapping on the bedroom door. Roarke must have heard it too, for they both froze at the same time. Staring at each other, both recognised the look of disbelief each wore at the realisa-tion that they had responded to each other again. Yet there was no time to discuss it, for the tapping continued, man-aging to sound even more frantic.

'I'll get it.' Feeling self-conscious, Ginny clambered awkwardly off Roarke and scrambled to her feet. Smooth-ing her nightdress down, she composed herself as best she could before going to answer the door. A glance back at the bed showed that Roarke had vanished, then moments later she heard the shower running.

Taking a deep breath she opened the door, and gasped at the sight of her sister standing outside. 'Lucy!' she exclaimed in surprised delight.

Lucy, however, looked ill at ease, constantly glancing over her shoulder—and Ginny instantly knew what she was afraid of. Grasping her by the arm, she pulled her sister inside and hastily shut the door.

She was so pleased to see her younger sibling that she immediately enveloped her in a hug. 'It's so good to see you! I've missed you so much,' she declared in a voice thick with emotion, and only then became aware that her sister hadn't responded. Her heart sank as she realised she could have misinterpreted her sister's reason for being there. Lucy might well feel as James did, which wouldn't be so surprising. Bracing herself for rejection, she released her sister and stepped back.

'Sorry. You probably didn't come here for a family reunion at all,' she apologised uncomfortably. 'I got a little ahead of things,' she added with a laugh that teetered off-key.

Lucy's expression immediately became contrite. 'No, no, don't be silly. That was exactly what I came for, but I wasn't sure that you wanted to see me!'

'Not want to see you!' Ginny exclaimed in astonishment. 'Lucy, not a day has passed when I haven't wished I could see you.'

'I missed you, too,' Lucy confessed, and this time it was she who threw her arms around her sister. They shared laughter and brushed away a tear, and then Ginny held Lucy away from her.

'Let me look at you. You've grown so, I would hardly have recognised you.' Lucy had turned from a gangling youngster into a beautiful young woman of eighteen.

Just at that moment the bathroom door opened and Roarke stepped out. He wore nothing but a towel and a smile. The sight of him took Ginny's breath away and knotted her stomach. She could feel telltale warmth invading her cheeks.

'Ladies.' Roarke greeted them with charming panache, considering the situation.

Ginny decided to ignore his lack of clothes—as much as she could, anyway. 'Lucy, this is Roarke. James is marrying his sister. Roarke, my sister Lucy.'

Roarke's grin was dashing. 'Pleased to meet you, Lucy. Let me get some clothes on, and then we can talk and spare Ginny's blushes.' With which taunting statement he crossed the room and vanished into his dressing-room.

Lucy giggled, and Ginny rolled her eyes. 'Don't encourage him!'

'No, I'll leave that to you,' her sister returned, tongue-in-cheek. 'Thank goodness your taste in men has improved. I never did like Mark,' she added seriously, surprising Ginny.

'You didn't?' she asked falteringly.

Lucy pulled a face and shook her head. 'He was a phoney. I bet he didn't do half those things he said he did.'

Mark had bragged about where he had been and who he had met. Ginny had pretty soon discovered none of it was true. 'I wish you'd told me,' she drawled wryly. She could have saved herself a lot of grief.

'You wouldn't have believed me,' Lucy replied with a fatalistic shrug, and Ginny knew she was right.

'Probably not,' she conceded.

Lucy suddenly laughed brightly and gave Ginny a knowing look. 'But I like what I've seen of this one,' she said saucily, which made Ginny laugh. 'He's delicious.'

'And unavailable,' Ginny countered swiftly, surprised by the way her nerves had leapt at the notion that Lucy found Roarke attractive.

Roarke chose that moment to reappear, dressed in the trousers of his morning suit, white silk shirt and bow tie. Pausing by the couch, he retrieved the blanket and pillow he had used to make his bed.

'Come and sit down,' he invited.

'I can't stay long. Dad will be looking for me,' Lucy warned them, though she went to the couch, giving the bedding an odd look.

Roarke was equal to the unspoken question. 'We argued. I spent part of the night on the couch,' he admitted easily.

'Only part?' Lucy queried archly, and Roarke laughed, looking right at Ginny.

'We made up,' he said huskily, causing Ginny's cheeks to burn hotter.

'Making up's the best part,' Lucy agreed flirtatiously.

Roarke dumped the bedding on the bed and took one of the chairs whilst Ginny joined her sister on the couch.

'I'm glad you didn't respond to Ginny the way your brother did,' Roarke observed, and Lucy sighed.

'It isn't easy going against a man like our father. James collapses under pressure, and there's no one who can exert pressure as well as Dad.'

Ginny had firsthand knowledge of that. 'I'm sorry I wasn't there to help.'

'You had to get out. I understood that.' Lucy immediately waved away the attempted apology. 'When Dad told us we weren't to see you or speak to you, it made me angry. Later, he said your name wasn't even to be mentioned, and I really hated him. I used to mention you all the time, just to annoy him. It was worth being sent to my room to see his face go red. You were my sister, and nothing he said or did was going to change that. I'm really sorry I didn't speak to you last night, but he was watching, and if I'd attempted it he would have made Mum's life a misery. So I waited until this morning and snuck out before he did his rounds!' she finished with a spirited laugh.

Roarke grinned at her. 'Seems the women of your family are a strong-willed bunch. Could it have something to do with the hair?' Lucy's hair was red, too, if less vibrant than Ginny's. 'I'll have to watch what I say around you two.'

'Oh, I'm a kitten compared to Ginny,' Lucy contested. 'Just don't get in her way when she's really mad.'

'Lucy!'

'Well, it's true! You're by far the most passionate of us all!'

Ginny couldn't help her gaze drifting to Roarke, saw in his eyes the acknowledgement that he had already discovered the passionate side of her for himself. She hadn't wanted it to resurface, but it had. Twice now she had found herself a captive of her sensual response to this man, and she didn't like it. It wasn't part of her plan.

'I'm not the person I was, Lucy,' she denied, turning back to her sister. 'I learned the hard way not to be so foolish. The world didn't stand still these last eight years.'

'Why didn't you keep in touch?'

'Not because the Brigadier told me not to, but because I thought you would fare better if I stayed away.'

'You were right in a way, it was better—until recently,' Lucy confirmed, then her expression clouded.

Ginny's stomach knotted. 'What happened?'

Lucy opened her mouth to explain, but the clock on the mantelpiece began to chime, and she got to her feet quickly. 'Half past eight already! I can't talk any more now, Ginny. Dad asked for breakfast in his room for all of us, so I'd better go. We'll talk again, I promise,' she insisted as she made her way to the door.

'Let me make sure the coast is clear,' Roarke commanded, taking a swift look up and down the hall. 'It's OK.'

The two women hugged each other swiftly, and then Lucy left, walking briskly down the hall. At the corner she glanced back and waved, then she was gone.

'Nice girl,' Roarke remarked as he shut the door again. 'I find it amusing that a man like Sir Martin, who likes to throw his weight around, should have two daughters strong enough to fight him. He can't have expected that his son would be the weaker one.'

'He should have done. The red hair comes from his side of the family. James takes after our mother,' Ginny responded with heavy irony, and their eyes met as they shared the joke. However, when the laughter faded, they found themselves remembering what it was that Lucy's arrival had interrupted, and the air around them began to crackle with electricity.

Ginny licked her lips and took the bull by the horns. 'What happened earlier... That was a mistake,' she declared firmly.

Roarke had no trouble following her. 'I couldn't agree with you more.'

She folded her arms protectively. 'I'll play the part as I promised, but we'll have to keep our distance. I don't intend for anything to happen a third time.'

'I'm with you all the way, sweetheart. Finding myself physically attracted to you wasn't on the cards for me, either,' he acknowledged. 'Discovering this unexpected fire in you doesn't help. It would have been better if that ice in your blood hadn't melted!'

'I never had ice in my blood. That was your invention. If I appeared frosty, it was because I didn't like you.'

'Well, sweetheart, we would both have been better served if you'd continued to dislike me,' Roarke shot back.

'I never stopped. In fact, right now, I dislike you every bit as much as I ever did!' Ginny returned fire swiftly.

'Then why didn't you put up more of a fight when I kissed you?' he wanted to know, incurring her wrath.

Her lips parted in an angry gasp. 'Are you suggesting this is all my fault? You should learn to keep your hands to yourself!'

His lips twisted into a mocking smile. 'I would, if you didn't keep responding to me!'

Green eyes narrowed wrathfully. 'So it is my fault!'

'I didn't say that.'

'Not in so many words, but I got the message. Damn, none of this would be happening if you hadn't kissed me last night!' she exclaimed accusingly.

'Cut it out, Ginny. Neither of us expected the response we got. Besides, whilst we're on the subject, who was exploring whose body no more than an hour ago?'

Of course she had no answer to that. Roarke had been asleep. It had been all her own idea. All she could do was draw herself up to her full height. 'Thank you for throwing that back in my face!'

Roarke took an impatient step towards her, which she countered by taking a step back. 'I wasn't about to touch you,' he protested irritably.

'I wasn't taking the chance!'

'Now you're just being ridiculous. I have no intention of touching you...in that way...ever again,' Roarke snapped back testily.

'You can't know how happy I am to hear that!' Ginny snorted, fully aware that she was overreacting, but not seeming to be able to stop.

'Oh, for the love of God! Nobody has to take all the blame. We're both at fault. It turns out this response we have to each other isn't going to vanish as easily as we expected. We didn't ask for it, but we have to deal with it. We can't expect someone to always bang or knock on a door to stop us doing something rash.'

Ginny knew he was right. They had to get control of the situation. 'OK. No kissing, no touching—no anything. We keep our distance from now on.' How hard could it be? They would be leaving the next day, so there was something like twenty-four hours for them to get through. They could do this. All it would take was self-discipline.

'Fine,' Roarke agreed, dragging a hand through his hair.

'OK, then,' Ginny retorted, facing up to him.

An uneasy silence fell, during which time each observed the other warily. This was a new situation, and neither wanted to precipitate another incident. Roarke's eyes dropped, taking in her apparel.

'You can help by putting some clothes on, or are you going to stay like that all day?' he asked sarcastically, waving a hand at her nightdress.

Not for the first time, she was tempted to hit him. 'Of course not! I'm going to shower and change, and then we're going to see your sister,' she exclaimed, putting action to the words by heading for her dressing room. 'And if I don't murder you before the day is out, you can consider yourself lucky!' she added, before vanishing inside.

Of all the nerve, she thought, as she collected together underwear and the dress she intended to wear for the wedding. She had been respectably covered in her nightdress, whilst he had wandered around in a towel. Talk about a double standard. Obviously she had become Eve, the temptress, and he was the poor hapless male. Hah!

Gathering up her things, she re-entered the bedroom. Roarke was on the telephone. Ginny crossed to the bathroom without looking directly at him, but she felt his eyes on her all the way. Her spine tingled. Only with the bathroom door shut did the feeling go away. Setting her clothes down and hanging her dress on the door, she stripped off her nightdress and stepped into the shower. The warm water was refreshing and she stood under it, savouring the pleasure.

However, as she stood there, thoughts of Roarke and her response to him trickled back into her mind. There was no denying the response, but how had it happened? She would have bet anything that she would never feel anything for him. She disliked him and his attitude to women. Or did she...?

Hadn't it always been the case that she disliked his attitude to women more than she disliked him? When she had first met him, hadn't there been a moment when he had set her nerves jangling? Before she remembered his reputation, and that he was exactly the kind of man she was determined to avoid?

If she was honest with herself, then she knew that attraction didn't just flare up. It had to have been there, unacknowledged. They had been fighting for so long that neither realised it had masked what they were now discovering was a pretty powerful mutual attraction. It had been hidden because neither wanted to acknowledge a response to the other. They called it dislike and fought like cat and dog. Now the blinkers were gone and they were left to face the passion.

Which they still didn't want, because they were the same people. Only it was going to be harder to ignore, because they had had a taste of what it could be like. Temptation hovered, however inconveniently. At least things hadn't gone too far. They could retrieve the situation. That, at least, they were agreed upon.

With renewed determination Ginny washed, then dried herself on the softest towel she had ever held, and dressed in the pale lavender shift dress. She emerged from the bathroom feeling much more confident, only to have that confidence tilted dangerously by the view she had of Roarke standing at the dressing table combing his hair. The action was stretching the cloth of his silk shirt over powerful shoulder muscles, and that reminded her of what he had felt like to touch. Her mouth went dry.

'Something wrong?'

Roarke's eyes met hers in the mirror, and she hastily shook her head. 'I was just wondering what I did with my shoes,' she lied, giving herself a mental ticking-off for allowing the erotic thought to enter her head. The few seconds it took her to retrieve her far from lost shoes allowed her to regain her composure.

'Will your mother be with your sister?' Ginny asked in concern, fixing tiny diamond studs to her ears as she emerged from the dressing room.

Roarke laughed at the mere idea. 'Mother never puts in an appearance until lunchtime. She'll make a concession today, but I still don't expect her to emerge before eleven. We should be able to get a short time alone with Caroline before her bridesmaids turn up, if we're quick. Are you ready?'

'Yes. I won't put on the matching jacket until we leave for the church,' Ginny added as they headed out of the door.

'I'm resisting wearing the rest of this monkey suit until the last minute myself,' Roarke remarked wryly.

'Morning dress suits you,' she felt compelled to admit.

He quirked an eyebrow at her. 'Are compliments allowed under the rules?'

'I've complimented you before,' Ginny pointed out, which caused him to grin.

'But that was before we discovered we were attracted to each other,' he countered, setting her nerves leaping.

Ginny winced. 'Comments like that are definitely out,' she declared.

'Hiding our heads in the sand isn't going to help.'

She knew that. All the same... 'Can we not discuss it right now?' she begged, hurrying to keep up with him. 'Where on earth is your sister's room—on the moon?'

'The other side of the house. Caroline prefers mountains to water. She has a morbid fear of it.'

'That's a shame!'

'It's a shame somebody didn't drown her father. He was the individual whose idea of teaching her to swim was to chuck her in the deep end!' Roarke explained, and clearly he had no love for his ex-stepfather.

Ginny felt a sympathetic anger too. 'He was husband number two, I take it?'

'Correct. He was a flautist of international renown, but a dead loss as a human being. Fortunately, Caroline inherited his talent and not his ego. Here we are.'

Roarke halted at a door and tapped out a particular series of knocks. Catching Ginny watching him in amazement, he shrugged. 'We all have our own knocks—that way, the person whose room it is knows whether to answer or not.'

Ginny's lips twitched. 'Who were you trying to avoid?'

'Mother, mostly.' He grinned unrepentantly, and looked so boyishly handsome that her heart skipped a beat and her breathing went awry.

Something must have shown on her face, for he frowned. 'You OK?'

'A touch of indigestion,' she invented hastily.

That brought his brows arcing. 'You haven't eaten anything.'

There were times when his persistence could be downright irritating. 'Must be an empty stomach, then,' Ginny countered and was relieved to hear the door open.

'Honestly, Roarke, where have you been? I expected you earlier,' Caroline complained as she looked out, then caught sight of Ginny. 'Oh!'

Roarke stepped forward, hustling his sister away from

the door and back into her room. 'Caro, meet Ginny. Ginny, Caro.' He introduced them to each other as he did so.

'Pleased to meet you,' Ginny murmured politely, following them in and shutting the door at a jerk of the head from Roarke.

'Likewise,' Caroline returned, then pulled an angry face at her brother and slapped his hands away. 'Stop it!'

Roarke held up his hands repentantly, then bent and kissed her cheek. 'Sorry, darling, but we need to speak to you alone, and we don't want to be seen coming in here.'

'Why? What have you done?' she asked suspiciously.

Roarke straightened up. 'Why do you always assume I've done something?'

'Because you're a rogue,' Caroline observed simply.

Unsure how long this sibling badinage was likely to go on for, Ginny cleared her throat to attract their attention. Caroline was instantly contrite.

'Now look what we've done. We're upsetting your... friend.' The fractional hesitation was glossed over by a friendly smile.

'Ginny is more than a friend,' Roarke amended, and his sister glared at him.

'I was trying to be polite,' she hissed through her teeth.

'There's no need to worry,' Ginny interrupted. 'I'm used to your brother's shortcomings,' she added sweetly.

Caroline frowned. 'I don't understand.'

'No, but you will,' her brother declared, leading her by the arm to a nearby chair and urging her to sit. 'We want to talk to you about Sir Martin.'

The other woman couldn't have been more surprised. 'Sir Martin? What about him?'

'For one thing, Ginny is his daughter,' Roarke said without preamble, and his sister blinked.

'His daughter? But I thought…' The sentence tailed off as she looked steadily at Ginny.

'He only had one?' Ginny finished for her, taking the spare seat. 'That's because he disowned me many years ago. I was shown the door and told never to darken it again, because I chose to follow my own path. I took my mother's maiden name, Harte.'

Caroline had been studying her closely. 'Yes, now that you mention it, I can see the likeness between you and Lucy.'

'Please don't think I'm here to try and talk you out of a marriage, because I'm not. Your brother asked me to tell you something about the family you're marrying into, that's all. You see, the Brigadier, my…father, is a very…forceful man.'

Caroline looked from her brother to Ginny, and just the faintest of smiles curled at the outer edges of her lips. 'I've always thought of him as a bully,' she remarked, taking the wind right out of their sails.

'You do?' Ginny gasped in amazement.

'I never thought of calling him the Brigadier, but it's a good name for him,' Caroline added with a wry laugh, before looking at Ginny. 'It was good of you to come, but you didn't have to. I've known for a long time just the sort of man Sir Martin is. Your brother James is a decent man, but whenever he comes into contact with his father, he changes. He's intimidated and he knows it, so he becomes angry and aggressive. He isn't the man his father would have him be, and he has anxiety attacks because of it. Yet when he's with me he's a different person, softer, calmer. James is a talented man. He's a brilliant watercolourist, did you know?'

Ginny shook her head. 'No, I didn't. What my father deemed as "sissy subjects" were banned in our house.'

A determined look settled on Caroline's face. 'Maybe in his house, but not in mine. I love James, and I fully intend to get him away from your father's influence just as soon as we are married.'

The unexpected declaration, said with such determination, brought a lump to Ginny's throat. She stared at her soon to be sister-in-law with growing respect. 'So you do love him.'

Caroline frowned a little. 'I wouldn't be marrying him if I didn't. Does that surprise you?'

'No,' Ginny denied hastily. 'It was suggested to me that you might be marrying him to get away from your mother,' she added, with a pointed look at Roarke.

'You'll pay for that,' he promised, and Ginny raised her eyebrows.

'Oh? And just how do you propose to do that?'

'I'll think of something.'

Following the exchange with interest, Caroline laughed. 'Roarke has this thing about love and marriage. One doesn't exist and the other doesn't last.' She looked at her brother fondly. 'I wasn't too sure myself at one time, but I am now. Love exists, and marriages don't have to fail if you work at them. Our parents find it easier to flit from one to the other, because it's easier than making a proper commitment. They fail, but I don't intend to. You'll find you think the same yourself one day, Roarke.'

Her brother was quick to shake his head. 'I'm not looking for love,' he pronounced, which only made her smile broadly.

'Good, because that's just the time when you'll trip right over it. I wish I could be there to see the moment when you realise that old magic has got you too!'

Roarke laughed along with her. 'Never going to happen, darling,' he insisted, taking her hand and pulling her to her feet. 'We'd better be off. Time's getting on and you've got to get ready.' Taking her in his arms, he gave her a powerful hug. 'Be happy.'

'I intend to,' she responded in a watery voice when he released her.

On impulse, Ginny hugged her too. 'James is very lucky,' she said gruffly, knowing that her brother might just have found salvation.

'I'm the lucky one,' Caroline corrected. 'You must come and see us. I'll have Roarke give you our address.'

Ginny stepped back with a wince. 'You might want to check that out with James first, but thanks for the invitation. It was a kind thought.'

Looking troubled by Ginny's response, Caroline took her hands. 'I can't imagine what it must have been like to be cut off from your family. I know it would hurt me, so I'm sure it must have hurt you. But that's over now. Trust me, James will want to see you.'

Ginny didn't believe it, but she wouldn't spoil Caroline's day by saying so. 'Maybe you can work miracles.'

They were interrupted by a knock on the door.

'That will be my bridesmaids come to help me dress. Mother will be descending on me too, soon.'

'Which is our cue to leave,' Roarke said with heavy irony. 'See you in church, Caro.'

They left Caroline in the capable hands of her four bridesmaids and headed back the way they had come.

'I have to hand it to my little sister. She surprised me with that one,' Roarke commented.

'That's because she isn't a little sister any more. She grew up. Like Lucy. We think we know them, but we don't really. Do you think she could be right about James?'

'After this morning, it wouldn't surprise me. Have faith in Caro. If anyone can help your brother, she can.'

'Mmm, I liked her. In fact, the more I see of your family the more I like them. You're even likeable yourself when you're not being obnoxious,' Ginny admitted reluctantly.

'Ditto,' Roarke returned promptly, and their eyes met. Not for the first time sexual awareness ignited between them, and the air began to thicken. Ginny found it hard to look away, and when she did she still felt as if she had run a race.

They hadn't touched or anything like that. All they had done was look at each other, and that chemical reaction started all over again. It was getting ridiculous.

'Let's get some breakfast,' she suggested tersely, not because she was hungry but because right now she would rather not be alone with him. So far as she was concerned, the sooner this weekend was over the better.

CHAPTER SEVEN

THE wedding service was beautiful. The bride was radiant and the groom looked nervous, but that was how it should be. She and Roarke were seated on the bride's side of the church. If she glanced to her right she could see her parents and Lucy in the front pew but, so far as she could tell, nobody had looked her way. Doubtless her father had laid down the law again.

The church was packed with relatives and other well-wishers, which was why Ginny found herself pressed up close to Roarke's side. She had tried to make more room for herself, but that had only had the effect of brushing her thigh against his. A manoeuvre which had caused him to look at her mockingly and she had desisted. However, the warmth coming from him was impossible to ignore, as was the far too intoxicating scent of his cologne.

Just being close to him was turning her on, and she had known how it would be. That reckless side of her nature, which she had relentlessly suppressed for so long, was coming to the fore again. Her sensuality had come out of her self-imposed deep freeze and was being bombarded by signals it didn't want to ignore.

She was doing her best, though, but it didn't help that she still had a role to play. When the service was over, and they all rose to follow the bride and groom out of the church for the taking of photographs, she would have preferred to walk alone, but she became aware of Jenna watching them, and was forced to take Roarke's arm, holding on to it far more tightly than was comfortable.

Roarke glanced at her, brows raised questioningly, and she sighed, knowing he wanted to know why she was holding him when she had been the one to insist on no touching. 'We're being watched,' she explained in an undertone, and he nodded, placing his hand atop hers to add to the illusion, unwittingly sending her temperature rising.

They wandered outside with the rest, but there was scant relief for Ginny. To her dismay Roarke insisted she joined in all the family group photos.

'You're part of the family, even if only a few of us know it,' he informed her when she attempted to protest. 'You have more right than some to be here.'

To which she had no response. And seeing the annoyance on the Brigadier's face did make her feel better. Of course, she didn't move when the groom's family were called for, because that would raise some pretty difficult questions.

There was, however, no getting away from the traditional greeting of the guests by the bride and groom and their immediate families, when the guests moved on to the hotel where the wedding reception had been arranged. If anyone thought it odd that the bride should greet her as warmly as she did her brother, whilst the groom barely shook her hand, nobody remarked upon it.

Naturally, Jenna took advantage of the situation to kiss Roarke far too enthusiastically, which brought a dark look to Lewis Adams's face, despite the fact that Roarke pulled himself free almost immediately. At his side, Ginny could feel his anger and when it was her turn to shake hands with the woman, she gripped her hand tightly so that Jenna was forced to look at her.

'Do that again, Mrs Adams, and you'll be sorrier than you can possibly imagine,' Ginny promised softly, attaching a friendly smile to the words that didn't reach her eyes.

'I don't know what you mean!' Jenna protested her innocence, trying to free her hand without drawing attention to herself.

'I'm not Roarke, Jenna, and I have no qualms about calling a spade a spade,' Ginny had time to add before finally releasing the other woman and moving on.

This brought her to her sister, who gave her a swift smile and an even swifter shake of the hand. Sir Martin was next, and Ginny made no attempt to shake his hand. 'Brigadier,' she said coolly, before passing on to her mother.

Emily Beavis was patently nervous, and looked everywhere but directly at her eldest daughter, which saddened Ginny. 'James looked very handsome today, Mum. You must have been proud of him,' she said, willing her mother to say something, anything.

Her mother jumped, but at last she did meet her daughter's eyes. 'Oh, yes…I…er…'

'Emily!' Sir Martin's stern warning lashed out, making his wife blanch.

'Oh, dear!'

Ginny could have killed him for that, but she took pity on her mother and, defying the man standing by, she gave her a brief hug. 'I love you,' she whispered gruffly, then quickly turned away.

Her eyes were dazzled by unshed tears, and it was just as well that Roarke slipped an arm about her waist and guided her away from the group by the door, because she couldn't see where she was going.

'Here, take this.' He urged a glass into her hand, and Ginny took a bracing sip of what turned out to be a fine champagne.

'Sorry about that,' she apologised a little while later, once her composure had returned. 'I hate to see her so cowed, but I can't really remember her any other way.'

'Why doesn't she leave him?' Roarke asked the obvious question.

'Because he has her so much under his thumb, she can't do a thing without his approval. Besides, the family and her home is all she has. If she had any courage once, he's bullied it out of her by now,' Ginny answered dispiritedly.

'Just as well you got away from there when you did,' Roarke observed grimly.

'Amen to that,' she answered with a heartfelt sigh.

'So now all we have to do is make sure your sister Lucy breaks free too,' he went on, causing her to stare up at him.

'We?' she queried with a tiny frown.

'Did you think I was going to let you go into battle for her alone?' Roarke challenged, and Ginny's heart did a strange little flip-flop in her chest.

'It isn't your fight, Roarke,' she reminded him, at the same time feeling oddly unsettled inside.

'It is now,' he insisted calmly, and Ginny didn't know whether to be pleased or angry.

Her laugh sounded odd to her own ears. 'Because your sister married my brother?'

Roarke shook his head, and the look he held her eyes with was compelling. 'Because that man has done all I intend he should ever do to hurt you, sweetheart. What he does to your sister hurts you, and that's all I need to know. Got it?'

Oh, she got it all right, but she didn't believe it. He took her breath away. He made it sound as if how she felt was important to him, and she wasn't used to that. Not from anyone, least of all Roarke Adams. She had no idea what to say.

'Why are you doing this?' she had to ask, though her voice was a croak, her throat was so tight.

'Because somebody has to,' he responded forcefully.

Ginny drew in a very shaky breath. 'I'm having trouble seeing you as a white knight.'

Roarke's laugh was wry. 'That's because you've painted me as an unsavoury Lothario ever since you met me. If I did a good deed, you would have ignored it.'

He wasn't far off the mark, and that made Ginny feel uncomfortable. 'You're right, and I apologise. You aren't all bad.'

'Damned with faint praise,' he exclaimed in amusement.

She had to smile ruefully. 'It's hard to let go of the image I have of you.'

His brow quirked. 'That's the one of me bed-hopping and writing notes in a little black book?'

It did sound like a ridiculous stereotype put like that. 'It's more comfortable thinking of you that way,' she admitted reluctantly.

'I know what you mean,' Roarke put in feelingly. 'I'm trying to hold on to my image of you as a cold-blooded harridan, but this sexy redhead keeps getting in the way!'

The whole of her body seemed to jolt at his description of her, and her stomach knotted. She could feel heat flooding into her cheeks. 'Cut it out, Roarke!' she ordered thickly. 'I'm not…what you said!'

'Sweetheart, you should try looking at yourself from my point of view,' he drawled huskily, setting her nerves tingling like crazy.

She didn't dare when she was having her own problems. When he was just Roarke Adams, vile womaniser,

she could pigeonhole him and carry on her way. Since he
had become Roarke, the man who could make her blood
sing, she didn't know what to make of him, and he was
impossible to ignore. Now she also had to try and forget
the fact that he thought her sexy. They had come a long
way in a very short time, and the end result was far from
ideal.

At least she had recovered from the emotional turmoil
of the brief meeting with her mother. Which, now she
came to think of it, might have been his intention all
along. Proving yet again that he was not the man she had
always thought him. There were layers to him that she
had never suspected, and each time she uncovered one
her idea of him changed, making it impossible to dislike
him. It was very disconcerting, because her dislike of him
had been a fire wall behind which she had hidden. With
that removed, she was once more in danger of feeling the
heat of her sensuality.

Like now, for instance. Roarke wasn't watching her,
giving her the chance to observe him unobserved. There
were lines beside his eyes and mouth, which suggested he
laughed easily and often. She liked men who laughed. Her
father was a sober man, too full of his own importance to
damage his dignity by laughing. Roarke's eyes twinkled,
too, at thoughts he generally kept to himself. Physically,
he looked powerful, but she knew how gentle he could
be, and that was a big turn-on. There didn't seem to be
an inch of her that wasn't aware of every inch of him.
She had never experienced so strong a pull, and it was
downright scary.

'Have I grown another head?' The amused question
reached her ears and brought her out of her reverie.

Naturally she looked up and green eyes met grey. She
was getting a little more used to the thrill that went

through her whenever that happened, but it didn't stop her nerves from tingling.

'No, thank goodness. One of you is enough!' she returned with heavy irony.

His lips twitched. 'Really? I thought you might be memorising my features so you can dream about me later,' he countered equally mockingly.

'I don't need to do that. Your face is unforgettable. More likely to bring on a nightmare than a pleasant dream.'

'Now, that wasn't nice. It was also untrue,' Roarke dismissed easily, not in the least offended. 'You're no more afraid of me than I am of you. I know what gives you nightmares, remember, and I'm not it.'

'In that case, it's awfully big-headed of you to assume I'd dream about you,' she told him in her coolest tone, to which he merely laughed.

'Sweetheart, I doubt you can get me out of your head any more than I can get you out of mine, right now,' he remarked dryly, and she knew what he meant. He was occupying far too much of her thoughts.

'Well!' she exclaimed with false brightness. 'This isn't turning out at all the way I expected!'

'Oh, yeah!' Roarke agreed. 'Life has a way of knocking the ground out from under you all right.'

She grimaced at him helplessly. 'Why did you have to turn into a nice guy?'

He spread his hands. 'Why did you have to thaw out?'
Stalemate.

Ginny groaned. 'This is getting us nowhere.'

'Fighting the inevitable is generally a waste of time,' Roarke pointed out, and Ginny rounded on him.

'Nothing is inevitable. We still have a choice. I choose

to do nothing about it!' she insisted, and once again their gazes locked. An electric silence fell.

'How come I never noticed that your eyes are such a startling green before?' Roarke wanted to know. 'It would be very easy to drown in them.'

She knew the feeling. She only had to look into his to feel the same. 'I'll throw you a life preserver,' she returned a tad breathlessly.

'Hey, you two!' A voice right beside them made them both start. They looked round to find one of Roarke's brothers grinning at them. 'This isn't the time or place for what you two were contemplating! Besides, lunch is being served. The amount of electricity coming off both of you, you'll need to stoke the boiler or you might run out of steam just at the wrong moment!' he added, and walked away laughing and grinning from ear to ear.

'Thanks for the advice, Jack!' Roarke called after him, whilst Ginny stood there with beetroot-coloured cheeks. She was very much aware that others had heard what Jack had said, and they were smiling as they went past.

'Sorry about that,' Roarke apologised, taking her arm and joining in the exodus to the dining room. 'One day I expect him to grow up.'

'Why is it the ground never opens up and swallows you just when you really wish it would?' Ginny groaned, glancing round under her lashes. It came as no surprise to meet the Brigadier's inimitable stony look, and realise that he had overheard what Jack had said too. 'Oh, great!' she muttered. It never rained but it poured. Still, his opinion of her was so low, this would hardly make a difference.

'What's up?'

'The Brigadier heard everything.'

'Forget it. Some people have the unhappy knack of being where you least want them to be,' he passed it off, then shot her a look. 'Does it bother you that he heard?'

Ginny sighed. 'No…maybe a little. It's the child in me that somehow still hopes to win his approval. Not very rational, but that's the way it is.'

'Sweetheart, he's a man who knows the price of everything and the value of nothing. He won't change. He doesn't want to. It's his loss, but he'll never see it that way.'

Once again he astounded her with his perceptiveness. 'You've known him five minutes. How can you understand him so well?'

'Because I meet people just like him all the time,' Roarke returned with a faint shrug. 'They tend to have no sense of humour. It comes from taking themselves too seriously.'

'Something you could never be accused of,' she quipped, to which he chuckled.

'Life's hard enough without being able to find the funny side of it. Look at us, for instance. Now, that is funny.'

'Highly amusing, but I don't see you laughing,' Ginny pointed out sardonically.

'Somebody up there is having a huge joke at our expense, wouldn't you say? We've been skirmishing since the moment we met, and yet since yesterday what I want to do is get you alone somewhere, rip our clothes off and indulge in some indoor pursuit that I guarantee will give us both a great deal of pleasure.'

Instantly, Ginny's mind was filled with the vision exactly as he had described it, and it sent her temperature soaring. 'You don't go in for false modesty about your prowess, I notice,' she managed to say reasonably calmly, when she felt anything but calm.

Grey eyes glittered rakishly. 'I've had no complaints.'

'Yes, well, there's always a first time.'

Roarke laughed huskily. 'You'll be too out of breath to complain!'

She very nearly choked at that. It had to be the most downright arrogant thing he had ever said. 'I'd watch my step if I were you, or you'll be tripping over your ego!'

'I'm just telling it like it is.'

'Well, cut it out. You aren't helping to cool things down.'

He shrugged. 'The curse of an agile imagination. My mind insists on seeing the possibilities in vivid Technicolor.'

Ginny held up a cautionary hand. 'Don't tell me. I don't want to know. But you're right about one thing—the joke's on us. What I wouldn't give for a bargepole right now!' she added with wry amusement.

Roarke laughed softly, and the sound tingled its way along her nerves. She liked the sound of that laugh, which only went to prove she was losing her grip. Somebody up there was most certainly having the time of his life.

Several hours later, having consumed good food and good wine, with an appetite she hadn't expected, Ginny was feeling much more relaxed and at ease with the world. Fortunately, the seating arrangement had been traditional, so Ginny's family were on the top table, along with Roarke's. They themselves were on a table sufficiently far away to allow Ginny to forget them temporarily. The other guests at their table turned out to be distant cousins of Roarke's, and were a friendly group who had plenty of tales to tell about him, which he listened to with wry good humour, and kept the laughter bubbling.

They had just finished the inevitable speeches and

toasts, and now the wedding guests began to mingle once more and let their hair down. A band arrived and began playing dance music, and slowly couples began to filter on to the floor. Ginny found herself in constant demand by Roarke's male relatives, and for most of the next hour she was barely off the dance floor for long. Finally she pleaded exhaustion and returned to the table. Roarke was already there, though she had seen him dancing occasionally as she circled the floor.

He watched her flop into her chair and take a much needed drink from her glass of now tepid white wine. 'I had no idea you were so popular,' he observed coolly, and Ginny looked at his set expression and burst out laughing.

'I do believe you're jealous!' she gurgled, emboldened by the wine, though she was not even close to being tipsy.

'Not jealous, but I didn't find the sight of you being fondled by so many of my male relatives amusing,' he corrected smoothly, though Ginny thought she detected an edge to the words.

'I wasn't fondled, as you so delicately put it. I tell a lie—one of your uncles tried to grope me, but he had had too much to drink.' She pooh-poohed the idea immediately.

'You should have slapped his face,' Roarke declared, and she stared at him in total surprise.

'He was just being friendly.'

'He was being familiar, and I didn't like it.'

Her jaw dropped. 'Then you slap his face,' she rejoined smartly. 'Roarke, you're being ridiculous,' she added irritably, yet inside she experienced a tiny glow of satisfaction at his reaction. Which then confused her because of course she didn't want him to be jealous. He was nothing to her, their recently discovered attraction to each other notwithstanding.

He was not impressed. 'May I remind you you're supposed to be here with me?'

She was beginning to get annoyed. 'I am with you, Roarke, but you're starting to make me regret it,' she told him bluntly.

'Lovers' tiff?' Jenna's catty question took them both by surprise. They had been so involved in their argument that they hadn't heard her arrive.

Ginny swung round on her chair. 'Do you make a habit of eavesdropping on private conversations?' she charged the other woman, eyes flashing angrily.

'Actually, darling, your conversation doesn't interest me in the slightest. I came to ask Roarke to dance with me,' Jenna responded disdainfully. She gave him her most alluring smile. 'One dance, Roarke, for duty's sake. What possible harm could there be in that?' she cajoled, leaving him very little choice.

He rose to his feet with a tight smile. 'Never let it be said I refused to do my duty,' he said, standing back so that Jenna could precede him on to the floor. The other woman left with a wave of her fingers and a smug smile.

Ginny decided she was coming to seriously dislike Jenna Adams. The woman was trouble and, judging from Roarke's past experiences with her, there were few lengths to which she wouldn't go to get her man. However, there was very little she could get up to on the dance floor with all the family around them, so Ginny took the opportunity to visit the ladies' cloakroom. She was sitting at one of the vanity units when the door opened again and Lucy came in.

'I thought I would never get the chance to talk to you,'

Lucy said after the sisters had greeted each other with a hug. 'This is the one place even Dad wouldn't dare to go!' she added with a laugh.

Ginny laughed too, but she realised they didn't have much time, and there was something she desperately wanted to know. 'So, what were you going to tell me this morning? Why had things turned bad?'

Lucy sighed heavily. 'I met someone, Ginny. His name is Peter McMillan, and he's a law student in his final year. He's wonderful, and...I love him, Ginny, so much it hurts,' she said fervently, holding on to Ginny's hands.

Ginny could see where this was heading, and her heart sank. 'The Brigadier has other plans for you,' she said flatly.

'How do you know?' Lucy asked in surprise, and Ginny winced sympathetically.

'He told me so last night.'

'You've seen him?'

'Oh, yes,' Ginny confirmed wryly.

Lucy looked dispirited. 'He gave me this list of people he wants me to pick a husband from! I couldn't believe it. It's positively medieval!'

'Have you told him about Peter?' Ginny queried, and Lucy shook her head forcefully.

'I didn't dare to. I was afraid of what he might do. Peter wanted to confront him, but I knew that wouldn't work. Now Dad's turning on the pressure and I don't know what to do.'

Ginny knew, but it depended on one answer. 'Does Peter love you?'

Lucy's face took on a glow that would have made words unnecessary. 'Oh, yes. But he's not a rich man, and he doesn't come from a prominent family. Dad would never agree. Never. I thought about running away, but Peter shares with two other students. I had nowhere to go.'

'You do now,' Ginny corrected firmly. 'You must come to me.' She reached into her purse for a pen and snapped a tissue from the nearby box. She wrote quickly and handed the paper to her sister. 'This is my address. Hide it somewhere safe. As soon as you can, you must leave home and come to me. The Brigadier can't stop you. You're eighteen now, and legally free to leave home.'

The relief on Lucy's face was countered by a swift frown. 'But, Ginny, are you sure? If Dad found out he would be furious.'

'He can't do anything to me, Lucy,' she reassured immediately. 'You can stay with me as long as you like.'

Lucy bit her lip. 'I couldn't pay you much until I get a job, but I'm willing to try my hand at anything. Peter and I want to get a place of our own as soon as we can, but he has a student's loan to pay off, so it won't be anything grand.'

Ginny gave a swift shake of her head. 'You don't have to pay me anything. I just want you out of that house.'

'Will Roarke mind if I move in with you?' Lucy surprised her with the next question.

'Why on earth should he?' she asked, quite forgetting the role she was playing.

Lucy coloured up. 'Well, I mean… You two are used to being alone, aren't you?'

The penny dropped with an almighty clang. 'Ah! Actually, Lucy, things aren't quite what they seem. I'm just doing Roarke a favour,' she explained uncomfortably.

'Are you trying to tell me there's nothing between you?' Lucy asked in surprise, and Ginny nodded. To which her sister gave an unladylike snort of disbelief. 'I don't believe it. When you two are together there's a positive zing in the air. There's something putting that buzz in the air, and it isn't bees!'

That was something Ginny didn't want to hear. 'Roarke and I have been at loggerheads since we met. That's what you're picking up.'

Lucy tutted disappointedly. 'I didn't come down in the last shower of rain, you know, but if you don't want to talk about it, that's fine with me,' she declared airily, getting to her feet. 'I'd better go before he sends Mum out in search of me.' Bending, Lucy kissed Ginny's cheek. 'Thanks Ginny, you're a lifesaver.'

'That's what big sisters are for,' she retorted with a smile.

At the door, Lucy glanced back over her shoulder. 'I'll come as soon as I can.'

'I'll be waiting,' Ginny promised, and sank back with a sigh as the door closed behind her sister. It was going to be all right. Lucy was smart. She would play the dutiful daughter until the moment she left, and after that their father couldn't touch her.

She had Roarke to thank in the long run. If he hadn't asked for her help, she would probably never have known about James, and would never have seen Lucy. A lot had happened in the last few days, and mostly for the good. Now, if only she could help Roarke out with his father, she would have gone some way to balancing the scales. As for her attraction to Roarke himself, she was going to do her best not to think about it at all, because it was frightening in its intensity, and she had no idea how to deal with it. She was unsettled by what she was experiencing. On the one hand she didn't want it, yet on the other she knew that she had never wanted anything as much.

If there was a funny side to this turn of events, she just couldn't see it.

CHAPTER EIGHT

WHEN Ginny returned to their table some time later she discovered it was still empty, and began searching the crowd of dancers for Roarke. She found him without too much trouble—and the blonde head resting on his shoulder.

Anger shot through her like a rapier at the sight, and she had to restrain herself from rushing on to the floor and pulling Jenna off him physically. She reminded herself that Roarke was not hers, but that did little to quell the anger. All she could think was that the woman had no right to be acting so possessively and that she, Ginny, was going to put a stop to it once and for all.

How, she didn't know, until her roving gaze fell on Lewis Adams and saw that he was watching the couple too. His expression was tight, and she didn't have to be a mind-reader to know that he wasn't happy with the situation. Ginny knew it wasn't Roarke's fault that Lewis's wife was behaving so brazenly, but she wasn't so sure that Lewis would see it that way. She knew Roarke was against telling his father what had really happened with Jenna, for fear of making the situation worse, but Ginny credited the older man with more wisdom now. Someone had to put him straight, and if Roarke wouldn't do it, it fell to her to do so.

She had got no further than that when the man himself appeared before her. He smiled as he stood looking down at her, then held out his hand.

'I think we ought to go and break that up, don't you?' he suggested, taking her by surprise.

'Well…er…I was thinking the same thing myself,' she admitted, getting to her feet and eyeing him warily. 'Only…the situation might not be quite what you think.'

'And just what would that be?' he queried, ushering her the few yards to the dance floor and swinging her into his arms with decided panache.

Ginny licked her lips nervously. 'Roarke isn't…I mean, he wouldn't…' The words tailed off lamely as she wasn't sure how to proceed.

As it happened, Lewis Adams smiled kindly. 'I'm fully aware of what my son isn't doing or wouldn't do, Ginny,' he told her confidentially, and she blinked at him.

'You are?' she asked doubtfully.

'Oh, undoubtedly. I'm grateful that my son has better instincts when it comes to women than I do. You, my dear young woman, are the real McCoy, whilst Jenna is merely fool's gold. Myself being the fool,' he added with wry humour.

Her lips twitched. 'It wouldn't be polite of me to agree with you.'

'But to disagree would be a lie?' Roarke's father finished for her. 'You're quite right, of course. I did my son an injustice some years ago, and I fully intend to put that right. Firstly, though, I think it's about time I put you and Roarke out of my misery.' With which he steered her over to where his wife and son danced and tapped Roarke on the shoulder. 'Ready to change partners, son? It's time I took care of my wife. Come along, darling.'

Ginny and Roarke watched as he danced a scowling Jenna away from them, then they were jostled by a couple and he guided Ginny out of the way.

'We're creating a minor log jam here,' Roarke declared humorously, and Ginny eyed the crush dubiously.

'Let's go back,' she suggested, but Roarke caught hold of her hand and used it to twirl her into his arms.

'And waste a perfectly good dance floor? I think not,' he countered, giving her no chance to refuse.

This wasn't at all what Ginny had had in mind, but she could hardly create a scene over a dance. And dancing was all it was, she told herself firmly. Slowly, they began to circle the room.

'What was all that about with Dad?' Roarke asked curiously, and Ginny pulled away enough to look him in the eye.

'That was your father's way of telling you he's not as blind as you think. At least, not any more,' she told him seriously, and saw the message strike home in his eyes. Roarke tried to find his father amongst the dancers, but he had vanished from sight. He turned back to Ginny.

'What did you do?' he challenged suspiciously, and she shook her head.

'Nothing, honestly. He came to me and suggested he break you and Jenna up—in the nicest possible way, of course. From what he said, he's no longer fooled by her, and he's sorry he misjudged you.'

Roarke's eyes shone with affection for his parent. 'The old fox. He said that, did he?'

Ginny smiled, pleased for him. 'Not in so many words, but I could read between the lines. I won't steal his thunder. Anything else you want to know, you'll have to take up with him.'

'I will, just as soon as the time is right,' he confirmed, then held her gaze, looking deeply into her eyes as if searching for something. 'You're something of a lucky charm, Ginny Harte,' he murmured softly, but she shook her head.

'There's nothing the least bit magical about me.'

His brows curved upwards. 'Then how come it feels as if you're casting a spell over me?'

Her nerves leapt, and her pulse started to beat just that little bit faster. 'That's indigestion from too much rich food,' she retorted, making him laugh.

'I can handle the food, it's you I'm worried about.'

Tiny tingles were being set off along her nerve-endings. 'I'm no threat,' she countered huskily, vitally aware that being this close to him was undermining her resolve to keep her cool. The warmth coming off him was heating her blood.

Still his eyes searched hers and she was unable to look away as he sighed. 'Maybe not to world peace, but my sanity is in real danger.'

Her throat closed over, for the banked fires in his eyes told her he was feeling just the same as she was. Together they were combustible, and it was happening so fast it took her breath away.

'Then let me go,' she suggested tightly, though her whole body was sending out the message that it wanted to be closer, not farther away.

'Something tells me that will be impossible unless you walk away,' he confessed, and her stomach tightened as desire flared inside her.

Her brain knew the right thing to do, the safe thing, but it reacted sluggishly, unlike her senses, which were going into overdrive. Walk away? When it came to doing that, she was in the same boat as Roarke. She didn't have the strength to do it right now. In a moment of perfect clarity, Ginny knew that there was only one thing she wanted to do. She would worry about the consequences later, but right now she made her choice and moved that fraction closer to rest her head on his shoulder, her arms rising to encircle his neck. Beside her she felt Roarke take in a deep lungful of air, and then his arms tightened round her. Her eyelids dropped, closing out the world.

They danced on as one slow song changed to another. Their bodies moved, touching just enough to tantalise. Ginny breathed in the aroma of his cologne, which made a heady potion blended with his own male scent. The brush of his hand tracing lazy patterns up and down her spine was totally alluring, and in response her hand sought his nape, her fingers caressing up into his lush dark hair in combing strokes.

And all the while they danced she could feel his body hardening, responding to the stimulus, whilst her own was going into meltdown. She hadn't wanted this, she told herself. Lord knew it was the very last thing she had wanted, and yet she couldn't seem to stop herself craving more. It felt so good, how could it be wrong?

A little while later the music changed to a faster tempo, and they were reluctantly forced to move apart. Ginny glanced into eyes as stormy as she knew hers must be. Tempestuous forces had been created, and were barely leashed. Neither had wanted the dance to end and that was why, when Roarke took her hand, she allowed him to lead her off the floor and out into the night without a word of protest.

There were extensive gardens surrounding the hotel and Roarke followed a meandering path, eventually stepping off it into the shadows round the bole of a tree. Leaning back against the trunk, he drew Ginny towards him. The freshness of the clear air brought with it a momentary return to sanity and she resisted, pressing her hands against his shoulders.

'We shouldn't be doing this,' she protested, though there was little force behind it.

Roarke continued to urge her closer. 'I know. This is the last thing I expected or wanted. I must be crazy, but what the hell…' He began to lower his head.

'No, Roarke,' Ginny commanded weakly as his lips hovered over hers. 'I don't…' The words were cut off as his mouth claimed hers with a devastating passion, and her resistance vanished like dust in the wind. A groan of satisfaction escaped her as her hands stopped pushing him away and clung on tightly instead.

The kiss was every bit as mind-blowing as the others they had shared, and it reinforced the strength of their attraction. Lost to the world, they were swept away by the passion they sparked in each other. One kiss was never going to be enough. They were caught in the grip of a fever, and the only cure was to allow it to run its course.

Finally, Roarke managed to drag his mouth from hers. Breathing heavily, he rested his forehead against hers and closed his eyes. 'If I don't stop now, I don't think I'll be able to,' he declared in a voice made thick by passion.

Ginny groaned, every bit as breathless herself. 'Why is this happening to us? What did we do to deserve it? I was happy disliking you!' She railed against the fate which had brought them together.

'You won't get an argument from me about that!' he agreed, planting a trail of kisses down her cheek to her jaw line.

Ginny's head tipped backwards, allowing him access to the tender skin of her throat. 'I didn't ask to want you this way!' she groaned achingly. It wasn't what she had planned. It wasn't fair.

Roarke's teeth nipped gently at her earlobe, making her

gasp and shiver. 'What have you done to me, you little witch? I can't seem to keep my hands to myself. You're like a drug, the more I have the more I want.'

Her hands had somehow found their way to his chest, delighting in the heat that scorched her fingers through his silk shirt. 'I know, but we have to stop,' she said vaguely, concentrating on freeing one of his shirt buttons so that her fingers could slip inside. His flesh was warm and firm, inviting her to explore further.

'God, that feels good,' Roarke groaned against her neck, his tongue darting out to taste her.

Ginny shivered, caught in the grip of an intense desire. She had never felt like this before. Not with Mark and definitely not Daniel. She froze. Daniel! His name was like a douche of cold water, cooling the fire in her blood. From somewhere she found the strength to wrench herself away.

'Oh, God! What am I doing?' she whispered in an agonised voice. She raised her head to look at Roarke, who stood watching her, breathing heavily. She shook her head slowly. 'This is wrong.'

Roarke dragged a hand through his hair. 'Not wrong, sweetheart, just damned unexpected,' he growled back. 'There's nothing wrong with a man and woman wanting each other.'

Ginny rubbed her forehead to ease the beginnings of a headache. 'But you're the wrong man, and I'm the wrong woman.'

That brought a twitch of humour to his lips. 'Obviously not. Nature seems to be telling us we're the right people, physically at least. Maybe we should listen to what we're being told.'

'And sleep with each other, you mean?'

'Sleeping comes later.'

She scowled at him 'You just couldn't resist that, could you?'

'Actually, it's you I'm finding impossible to resist. Experience tells me it isn't just going to go away, so ignoring it isn't going to work.'

Ginny had been reaching that conclusion herself. Words were easy to say, but they only had to look at each other to go up in flames! Her eyes met his, and even in the darkness she could see the intensity there. 'You seem to be taking this very calmly.'

His response to that was to take her hand and place it over his heart so that she could feel it racing. 'I'm not calm, Ginny, far from it. In fact, I'm as confused as I ever hope to be.'

'You're saying this has never happened to you before? I can't believe that,' she charged him mockingly and he grimaced.

'Laugh if you want to, but it's true. Finding myself wanting you this badly has knocked me for six. It isn't a feeling I'm familiar with. When I'm around you I can't seem to think straight. I only know I want to make love to you. You feel it too. We're caught in a fever, Ginny, and there's only one cure. We have to let it burn itself out.'

'It sounds so cold-blooded,' she said with a shiver that had nothing to do with coldness and everything to do with the idea of making love with him.

He laughed huskily. 'Believe me, sweetheart, our blood will be anything but cold. I'm not suggesting a long-term commitment. These things never last long. It will burn itself out quickly unless we try to ignore it. We wouldn't be hurting anyone.'

Ginny looked steadily into his eyes. 'And afterwards?'

'Normal service will be resumed. I have no doubts we'll be back to daggers drawn in no time.'

Ginny turned her back on him and took two paces away, needing the thinking room. She had to be crazy to even be thinking of doing it, but what he was suggesting made a strange kind of sense. It wouldn't be a love affair in the usual sense. All they needed was to drive the fever from their blood and turn things back to normal. No one need ever know.

'My choice?' she asked over her shoulder, and Roarke nodded.

'I leave the decision up to you.'

She chewed on her lip. 'You'd abide by my decision?'

He groaned audibly. 'I might want you with a certain amount of desperation, but I've never seduced a woman against her will, and I don't intend to start with you.'

Ginny shook her head in bewilderment. 'I've never met anyone like you. You've aggravated me constantly ever since we met, and yet...'

His teeth glittered as he grinned. 'You can't keep your hands off me?'

She sighed and winced. 'Something like that,' she agreed, then turned back to him. 'This has got to be the weirdest situation. I'm standing here actually considering sleeping with you, when only days ago I was having dinner with another man.' And planning to marry him—if he asked her.

That wasn't going to happen now. Not because Roarke figured in her future, but because her attraction to him was showing her that a marriage without love and desire was impossible. She was a woman with passion, and to contemplate ignoring those needs and settling for Daniel was wrong. She didn't love him, and certainly wasn't sexually attracted to him. Such a relationship would be a disaster. He deserved better—and so did she.

'Sweetheart, you can be damn sure we're no good to anyone else whilst we're wanting each other this way,' Roarke drawled with some of his old irony, uncannily echoing her own thoughts. 'Come on, let's head back before someone discovers we're missing and wants to know where we've been and what we've been doing. I'd hate to have to lie to my mother.'

Ginny laughed as he intended she should, and the tension which had been surrounding them eased considerably. 'She must know the kind of thing you get up to.'

They strolled back along the path. 'She imagines what I get up to; she doesn't know. I haven't talked to anyone about my relationships since I was in my teens. I once hurt a girl I liked very badly, by talking to someone who couldn't be trusted. She slapped my face in front of practically the whole school, and I deserved it.'

Ginny couldn't resist slipping her hand into his and squeezing it gently. 'You know, you really are a nice guy. Though it pains me to say it, I doubt I could go back to actively disliking you.'

Roarke glanced down at her quizzically. 'Your trouble is, you're not as frosty as you like to make out, which will make it impossible for me to see you as anything but warm-hearted. I used to enjoy taunting you in the office.'

She laughed softly. 'I know. What will we do now that we've started a mutual admiration society?'

He sent her a wolfish grin, the kind that curled her toes and set her heart tripping expectantly. 'Oh, we'll think of something to keep us amused. I have quite an imagination.'

It didn't sound to Ginny as if he was talking about verbal badinage, but she chose not to pursue it. For the moment the fires had been banked and it was easier to assume an appearance of calm.

Her thoughts were distracted not long afterwards by a sudden swell of noise from the front of the hotel, which separated itself into the sound of voices laughing and talking. As they rounded the side of the building, they could see the bride and groom were standing on the top of the entrance steps, clearly about to leave. As they joined the back of the group, Ginny could hear several voices urging Caroline to throw her bouquet. Laughing, she placed her hand over her eyes and launched the bouquet into the air with the other.

There were gasps and cries of 'Catch it!' but Ginny was so busy watching the arc it made that she didn't realise it was heading straight for her until almost the last second, when she raised her hands to protect her head—and caught the bouquet instead. Nobody could have been more surprised than she, but then she became aware of the pointed remarks about confetti and wedding bells which were being sent Roarke's way, and colour stormed into her cheeks. Instinctively, she looked around for someone more deserving to pass the flowers on to, but everyone was smiling at her and wishing her good fortune, so she could do nothing but hold on to it.

It really was a lovely bouquet, and smelled heavenly, she discovered when she buried her face in it to avoid having to look Roarke in the eye. Eventually, though, she had to look at him, to find him brushing off the comments with good humour. Sensing her watching him, he sent a questioning look her way.

'I'm sorry,' she apologised. 'I didn't mean to catch it. I thought it was going to hit me, so I put my hand up. I ought to have ducked.'

He grinned. 'If you'd done that, I would have caught

it instead. Something tells me Caroline knew what she was doing,' he added thoughtfully.

Ginny looked startled. 'You mean she threw it our way deliberately? Why?'

'Because people who are happy themselves want to see others find happiness the same way. She obviously thinks we should get married,' Roarke explained sardonically.

'That would be a sure-fire recipe for disaster. We're simply not compatible.' Ginny had the answer to that.

'We're not totally incompatible, either. In some areas we appear to be getting along like a house on fire,' he corrected wryly.

A chauffeur-driven car drew up outside the hotel, and that was the happy couple's cue to make their escape. They did so in a shower of confetti, and then they were in the car and being driven off to start their honeymoon. As ever, a faint sense of anticlimax settled over the party, and they slowly made their way back inside. However, it was not long before the younger family members were dancing, and the level of noise rose as the celebration got under way again. It showed every possibility of continuing long into the night.

By unspoken agreement Ginny and Roarke did not dance again, but spent the next few hours chatting with various members of his family. Though she had only met them briefly, Ginny knew she would miss them, for they had made her welcome with a kindness she was not familiar with. At least now she had had a glimpse of what a real family could be like, and that was what she wanted for herself.

Around midnight Ginny began to feel the effects of the long, eventful day, and when she stifled yet another yawn Roarke suggested they should leave. They made their farewells, and headed for the door. Ginny would have liked to have said a few words to her mother and sister, but the Brigadier had them under his watchful eye, and she decided it would probably be best not to rock the boat any more than she had already today.

It didn't take long to be driven back to the house. Lights were on, but most of the family and guests were still at the hotel. Roarke led the way into the drawing room, unfastening his tie as he went and slipping it into his jacket pocket before releasing the neck buttons on his shirt. His hair was mussed up from where he had combed his fingers through it, and there was the shadow of beard on his jaw. To Ginny he looked handsome and sexy as hell.

'Fancy a nightcap?' he asked, strolling to the sideboard where a stunning array of drinks were set out. He turned to her, holding a cut glass brandy snifter in one hand and a bottle of Napoleon brandy in the other.

I fancy you more. The thought just slipped into her consciousness, accompanied by the impulse to close the distance between them, pull his head down to hers and share a kiss that would do more for her than any alcohol ever could.

Something of what she was thinking must have reached him, for suddenly there was an intense look in his eyes.

'Are you going to carry through on that?' he asked in a tellingly husky voice, making her nerves jump at his perspicacity.

'Carry through on what?' she countered, equally gruffly.

He took a step towards her. 'What you were just thinking.'

She swallowed to moisten a dry mouth. 'How do you know what I was thinking?'

'You have very expressive eyes, and though I might

not know the exact words, the gist is sending my pulse-rate rocketing.'

Ginny licked her lips, an act that drew his gaze and made her breath hitch in her throat. 'I'm sorry about that, because I don't know what I'm going to do. I haven't made up my mind.'

'It's interesting to know you can be as typically female as the next woman, but you pick a hell of a time to do it,' Roarke responded wryly.

'Unintentionally. I'm not a tease.' She wouldn't want him to think that. He didn't, because he smiled ruefully.

'I know you're not, Ginny. It's not in your nature.'

His certainty confused her. How could he be so sure? 'I've been accused of it before.'

'Only by people who don't know you as well as I do.' He dismissed the statement easily.

'You've scarcely known me longer yourself,' she felt compelled to point out, but he merely shook his head.

'Time has nothing to do with it. You can know a person your whole life and not know them at all. Then you can know somebody for twenty-four hours, and know them better than you know yourself. I feel I've come to know you very well, Ginny Harte, in the last couple of days.'

As she had come to know him. He had turned into a man she couldn't help being attracted to. Not for his good looks, although there was no denying that, but for the man he was. He had awakened her dormant sensuality without even trying, and she was beginning to realise she had been denying a vital part of herself for too long. Wanting Roarke was making her feel alive in a way she hadn't been for years. And it felt good. Maybe something was telling her it was time to kick over the traces and start living again. Dared she?

'Have I grown another head?' Roarke asked, reminding her she was staring, and her lips twitched.

'No, the one you've got is quite handsome enough.'

His brows rose. 'Sounds interesting. Tell me more,' he urged, with a rakish glint in his eye that taunted her to do something that would surprise him.

She knew what she wanted to do, and why shouldn't she? There was nothing stopping her but herself. Once upon a time nothing would have stopped her following her instincts. She had liked that person, and she could be her again—if she had the courage.

Just do it, Ginny, a small but insistent voice urged her, and suddenly she found herself taking one step and then another. Several more and she was standing in front of him. Her hand went to his neck, and for a moment their eyes met, his showing mild surprise. Then, a smile curving her lips, her gaze dropped to his. Rising on to her toes at the same time as her hand exerted just enough pressure to urge his head down, she set her mouth on his. Her tongue traced a silken caress over his lips, and they parted, allowing her entrance. With his hands full, there was nothing Roarke could do save surrender, and it gave Ginny a heady sense of power to take the initiative this way. She explored his mouth at leisure, her tongue seeking his and joining in a duel that set her pulse hammering and caused Roarke to moan low in his throat.

That was her cue to move away, and she did so with a certain amount of reluctance, stepping back from him. She looked at him steadily, seeing an arrested look in his eyes.

'What was that for?'

'I wanted to surprise you,' she answered simply.

He shook his head and laughed huskily. 'Sweetheart, you did more than that. You've made it virtually impossible for me to sleep tonight.'

She was instantly contrite. 'I'm sorry.'

'Don't be.' He waved that away. 'I could do with a few more surprises like that. Right now, though, I need that nightcap. How about you?'

'I'm going to go up and shower,' she refused.

'Well, you don't have to worry about using all the hot water. I'll be taking a cold shower later,' Roarke returned drolly.

Laughing softly, Ginny left him there and went upstairs to their room. She wasn't sorry she had kissed Roarke like that. It had felt good to follow her instincts again and act on impulse. He had taken it well, but she had known he would. She was getting to know him very well.

In their room, she found the maid had already been in to turn down the bed. Collecting her nightdress, she kicked off her shoes and padded into the bathroom. Stripping off her clothes, she stepped under the shower and let the warm water send down its soothing spray over her. She did a lot of her thinking in the shower, and tonight was no different. She had a lot to think about.

Her eyes had been well and truly opened by her response to Roarke, showing her in no uncertain terms that it was time she stopped fooling herself and started being true to herself. She was not the cold-blooded type. She had cut herself off from feeling, for fear of being hurt. At eighteen, in her inexperience, she had allowed passion to cloud her judgement, because she had so wanted to be loved. She had been an easy mark but she was no longer that girl. She was a woman in control of her life, who shouldn't be afraid to go with her instincts. By ignoring them she had almost made a serious mistake again. She would break the news to Daniel as soon as she returned home.

That decision brought with it an amazing sense of free-

dom. She felt as if she could breathe again. Now she had
to leave the past behind, look forward and see what came.
There was nothing stopping her from doing anything she
wanted to do. If getting involved with Roarke, even for a
brief moment, was a mistake, then it was hers to make.
As he said, they would be hurting nobody.

Taking a deep breath, she turned off the water and
stepped out, reaching for a luxuriously fluffy towel and
wrapping it around her. It was time to stop thinking and
act. She dried herself, slipped into her nightdress and tow-
elled her hair dry, finger-combing it into place.

When she stepped back into the bedroom, Roarke was
coming out of his dressing room. He was barefoot, wearing only his trousers. He had already taken the pillow and
cover from the bed and laid them out on the couch as he
had last night. It pleased her that he had taken nothing
for granted, but at the same time it piqued her that he had
assumed the decision was made. As she had told him, she
hadn't made up her mind.

'Feel better?' he asked casually, letting his eyes rove
over the feminine curves scarcely hidden beneath the
cream silk nightdress.

The way it sent a lick of fire over her skin made Ginny
feel as if the material wasn't there at all. Goose-bumps
chased their way over her flesh, and she felt her nipples
harden to sensitive points that thrust against the silk cov-
ering. Roarke could scarcely miss her response, and she
saw his chest rise as he took a deep breath, but although
his eyes flashed, he made no move to approach her.

Ginny cleared her throat. 'I'm cleaner, I don't know
about feeling better,' she told him openly, and amusement
danced across his face.

'That makes two of us. Somehow I get the feeling the
cold shower isn't going to count for very much. It's going

to be one hell of a long night!' he added as he headed for the bathroom. The door closed with a soft click behind him.

Ginny stared after him, knowing that it would be a long night for her too, with him lying only a few yards away. Especially as they both wanted something else. Her gaze swept round to the makeshift bed on the couch. This was ridiculous. There was no reason why they shouldn't have what they wanted. It wasn't a first date, for heaven's sake! They had known each other for months. The passion was new, but the spark had been there. They'd just interpreted it as something else.

Before she even realised she was doing it, she had gone to the couch and retrieved the pillow and cover and returned them to the bed. Of course, as soon as she had done it, her stomach turned over at the decision she had made, but she knew she wouldn't change it. There was no way, however, that she could simply sit on the bed waiting for him, so she went to the French window that opened on to a tiny balcony and stepped into the cool night shadows.

Pretending to look at the view, her ears were straining to hear the sounds from the other room. She heard the water stop and imagined him towelling himself off, then fastening another towel around his waist. He would reach for the light switch, then... Another soft click alerted her to the fact that he had left the bathroom. She tensed, imagining him finding the changed sleeping arrangements. Her heart started to race.

'Ginny?' The soft question made her glance round.

Roarke was standing by the end of the couch, watching her. He looked pretty much as she expected. His broad, tanned chest with its mat of dark silky hair stood out in contrast against the white towel hitched on his hips. He looked good enough to eat, and she was hungry—very hungry.

'Are you sure about this?' he asked, inclining his head towards the empty couch.

'Oh, yes,' she replied huskily, and it was all he needed to hear. He came to her, reaching out to gently cup her face with his hands. Grey eyes searched hers for any sign of doubt and found none.

Nevertheless, he still gave her an out. 'You know you can change your mind at any time. All you have to do is tell me to stop, and I will.'

The words made her heart turn over. No matter what she might have accused him of in the past, she had discovered he was an honourable man. She set her hands on his chest and instantly felt the reverberations of his quickened heartbeats. Any nervousness she had been feeling drained away. She was suddenly very sure of what she wanted.

'That isn't going to happen. Just take me to bed, Roarke,' she suggested in little more than a whisper. It brought a glint to his eyes and a smile to his lips.

Releasing her, he swept her up into his arms with breathtaking ease. Automatically Ginny's arms slipped around his neck. 'Never let it be said I refused a lady anything,' he retorted in amusement, but as he carried her to the bed the laughter faded, driven away by a look of such intensity it hid a powerful need.

Despite that, he laid her on the bed with infinite gentleness, and when he joined her, seconds later, the hand that traced the line of her cheek and jaw, then carried on down to the tender cord of her neck and graceful curving shoulder, held the faintest tremor. He was holding himself in check by supreme self-control, and he touched her as if she was made of the finest glass.

It was amazingly arousing to watch him as he followed his hand's journey along the curves and planes of her body. His gaze was so intense as he enjoyed each new discovery, that Ginny felt as if she were being burned by a touch as light as a feather. She knew even then that she knew nothing about pleasure. That what she had experienced had been little more than fumbling in the dark. This was pleasure delivered by a man who knew there was more to making love than reaching the end as quickly as possible.

She quivered as his hand brushed across her thighs, and caught her breath when he approached the swollen mounds of her breasts. He had started fires everywhere he touched, and she was burning up, so needy she could scarcely hold back a groan. She ached for him to touch her breasts, and arched into his hand as he cupped her. For one moment his eyes met hers, and it was like being touched by flame.

'I know,' he murmured thickly, then his thumb flicked across her engorged nipple, sending pleasure shooting through her body and dragging a moan from her lips.

She closed her eyes, but that only heightened the sensations as she felt his mouth close on her breast, his tongue laving her through the silk of her nightdress. She could no longer lie still, and her hand rose to his hair, slipping into the damp strands and clinging on as he drew her into his mouth and suckled. Her other hand found the sleek planes of his back and delighted in the glide of flesh on flesh.

Then his mouth sought the twin peak, delivering to it the same sweet torture it had given its mate before abandoning her breasts and seeking the honeyed sweetness of her mouth. Now she could sense the leashed desire in him. His tongue was a silken ravishment, seeking hers and demanding a response that left the pulses racing and breathing ragged. Only the need for air had him drawing back to look down into her flushed face and fevered eyes.

'I wanted this to last, but you're so intoxicating I don't think I can hold out for much longer,' he told her in a voice made husky by passion.

Ginny felt the same, but words were beyond her. Her answer was to reach down for the towel he wore and tug at it until he shifted his weight enough for her to pull it free and toss it aside. Roarke's nostrils flared as he got the message loud and clear. In return he took the hem of her nightdress and slid it upwards until finally he eased it free of her arms and sent it to join the towel.

Roarke's groan was echoed by her sigh of pleasure as he moved over her, taking his weight on his elbows. One powerful thigh nudged her legs apart, and to their mutual satisfaction he settled himself between them. Deep inside herself Ginny could feel the coils of desire growing ever tighter, climbing towards the ultimate goal, and she began to move restlessly beneath him as he teased her with kisses that stoked the fire but always left her wanting more.

All she could do was explore him with her hands, allowing her fingers to trace their way across taut flesh. He felt wonderful, but it was not enough. She wanted him inside her. Needed to feel the power of him dispelling the emptiness she had felt for so long. As if he was connected to her psychically, Roarke moved, slipping a hand between their bodies and into the valley of her thighs, seeking the core of her. His touch made her gasp and arch into him, leaving him in no doubt of her readiness.

With a groan he thrust into her, and Ginny's gasp was due to discomfort, not pleasure. They both stilled. There hadn't been anyone since Mark, and her body had tightened. Foolishly, she hadn't been prepared for it, but already her muscles were relaxing to accommodate him. Roarke raised his head to look at her, confusion clouding his eyes, and she felt him tensing his muscles in order to move away. That wasn't what she wanted at all, and she quickly folded her legs around him, holding him where he was.

'No. Don't stop,' she urged in a voice thick with passion.

Roarke gritted his teeth with the effort it was taking to hold still. 'I hurt you,' he declared tautly, but Ginny shook her head in vehement denial.

'No, you didn't. It was nothing. Please, Roarke, I want you. Don't stop now.'

He searched her eyes and what he saw there must have convinced him, for he began to move again. She could feel him holding back, taking care, but there was no need, and she moved against him, matching his rhythm, urging him on until, with a groan, the magnificent control he had been using crumpled and his thrusts became faster and deeper, seeking release. Ginny held on, her nails digging into the flesh of his back as the coils of pleasure spiralled upwards and finally climaxed in a white-hot explosion of pleasure. She cried out, and her cry was echoed by Roarke's as he joined her. She clung to him as a depth of satisfaction she had never experienced before held her in its grip. She felt as if she had shattered into a million tiny pieces and was being put back together again better than before.

When she finally floated down to earth, her body was drained. She had no energy to move and her eyelids were weighted. She felt Roarke slide off her, and wanted to protest, but no words passed her lips. Then she was being moved, and the last thing she remembered before sleep claimed her was Roarke's arms slipping round her.

CHAPTER NINE

GINNY sighed and drifted into wakefulness. She stretched and winced slightly as seldom used muscles protested. However, recalling the cause of this morning's stiffness, a reminiscent smile slowly curved her lips. Last night had been—out of this world. Making love with Roarke had taken her to heights she hadn't realised it was possible to reach. It had been amazing, exciting, and...she wouldn't at all mind doing it again.

With which thought in mind she rolled over, only to discover the other side of the bed was empty. Frowning, she came up on her elbow and swept her hair out of her eyes so that she could search the room. Roarke was just coming out of his dressing room, pulling a lightweight argyle sweater over his head. Settling it over the denims he was already wearing, he finger-combed his hair back into place.

She had always thought he looked good in formal clothes, but he was just as gorgeous in casual wear. The jeans moulded his legs, emphasising the muscles, whilst the sweater outlined the chest she had come to know rather well. She experienced a stab of disappointment that he was already up and dressed.

'Why didn't you wake me?' she asked, with just the faintest of pouts.

Roarke glanced over at her and a smile curved his lips. He immediately came over to the bed and sat down on the edge. Lowering his head, he took her lips in a long

147

lingering kiss, which went some way to appeasing her disappointment, drawing back with obvious reluctance, before the smouldering embers of their passion could be reignited.

'Good morning,' he greeted gruffly.

'Good morning,' Ginny returned equally gruffly.

Grey eyes quartered her face, and he brushed his knuckles gently over her cheek. 'How do you feel?'

'Pleasantly exhausted,' she responded, then grinned. 'But I have amazing recuperative powers,' she added suggestively, making him laugh softly.

'That's good to know, sweetheart, but that isn't exactly what I meant,' Roarke returned, holding her gaze. 'It had been a while for you, hadn't it?'

Faint colour washed into her cheeks at the unexpected remark. She had forgotten those brief moments of discomfort, and thought he had too. She instinctively distanced herself mentally. 'You were disappointed,' she declared flatly, feeling foolish, but Roarke was quick to correct her error.

'Nothing about you disappoints me, Ginny. Far from it. I only mentioned it because it was something I hadn't expected. It worried me that I could have been too rough, and hurt you.'

She relaxed again. 'Oh. I see. Well, let me tell you, Mr Adams, you didn't hurt me at all,' she told him honestly, and was faintly surprised to see relief flash across his face. His concern made her feel warm and bubbly inside. She wasn't used to being worried over.

'That's good, but I wish I'd known beforehand. I would have taken more care.'

More care? She couldn't help laughing. 'More care?

Roarke, you couldn't possibly have taken more care than you did.'

'So, what happened? Were all the men out there blind?' he teased, more like his usual self.

Ginny sighed. 'No. It was me. After Mark, I wasn't about to rush into anything,' she admitted, surprising him again.

'There's been no one since Mark?' he repeated in disbelief, and her shrug was just a little diffident. She didn't care to recall how stupid she had been.

'I made a fool of myself over him, confusing desire with love. The only way to make sure it didn't happen again was to keep all men at bay. When you've been burned, you learn to steer clear of the fire.' It was a philosophy which had worked well over the years, protecting her.

'OK, I can understand that. So why me? Why now?' Roarke asked curiously.

She could have said nothing, but she had already said so much, there was no point in hiding the truth. 'Because you're the only man who's ever made me want to change my mind.' She told the simple truth.

'Then I'm honoured,' he responded with an unexpected degree of sincerity, causing her heart to give a tiny lurch.

Feeling oddly emotional, Ginny had to make light of it or do something silly like burst into tears. 'You should be. The truth is, I'm under no illusion this time. You're here and I want you and, try as I might, I couldn't find a convincing reason not to have you.'

That brought a glint to his eye. 'You tried, though?'

Her laughter was openly flirtatious. 'Oh, yes. I didn't want sex rearing its ugly head and cluttering up my life, but if last night is anything to go by, I made the right choice.'

'I'm glad you were satisfied.'

Ginny reached out and trailed a finger along the V neck of his sweater. 'I was satisfied last night, but this morning… You should have woken me. Why didn't you?'

'Oh, I wanted to, believe me. You don't know how hard it was to keep my hands to myself and crawl out of this bed. All I wanted to do was kiss you awake and lose myself in you again. However, I thought you needed the sleep more, and the noble thing to do was leave you alone.'

'For future reference, I'm not that bothered about nobility,' Ginny told him wryly. 'So why don't you come back to bed?' she suggested with a winsome smile.

Roarke groaned but resisted temptation. 'I have to be crazy to pass up an offer like that, but I must. We don't have much time, and I want to speak to my father before he leaves this morning.'

She was disappointed, but she understood. 'Then what are you doing wasting time here? Go and find him. There will be other mornings.' Their desire for each other was not to be satisfied so quickly.

Grey eyes gleamed wickedly. 'You're right, and I shall be looking forward to every one of them. Last night was not the end, only the beginning. Now, I'd better go before my resolve weakens. I'll see you in a little while.'

He pressed a fleeting kiss on her lips then left the room. Ginny sighed wistfully. It was funny how things turned out. Nothing about this weekend had gone the way she expected, and yet it couldn't have turned out better. She had found her family again, and for that alone everything that had happened would have been worth it. Even running into her father.

And then there was Roarke. Neither of them would have bet on this happening, that they would end up in bed together. Yet she wasn't sorry. For the first time in a long time she felt as if she was truly herself again. The Ginny who knew what she wanted and went for it, unafraid.

She was older and wiser now. This time she wasn't going to mistake desire for love. It would be an affair, that was all. There was no love on either side, just a powerful desire. When it was over, she would walk away with her pride intact. There were no false promises, no impossible demands. They wanted each other, and they would enjoy every moment for as long as it lasted.

It was incredibly heady to feel free of the past, and Ginny lay there basking in the newness of it. But eventually her stomach started to rumble and she began to think of food instead of what she might be doing if Roarke was still here. Sitting up, she reached for the travel clock she had set on the bedside table and was startled to find it was getting on for eleven o'clock in the morning.

'Yipes!' she exclaimed, thinking of all the things she had to do before she could eat. Galvanised into action, Ginny flung back the covers, scrambled from the bed and hurried into the bathroom.

If either of them had thought that one week or even one month would see their passion for each other diminish, they would have been wrong. Six weeks after their return from the wedding, the attraction between them was as strong as it ever was. In fact, Ginny almost felt as if it was stronger.

As for herself and Roarke, they were virtually inseparable these days. At work they remained professional, but they no longer had the verbal battles everyone expected, which was causing even more talk amongst the staff. Ginny found herself being watched, and she knew they were being talked about, but it didn't bother her. She was happy, and breezed through even the most hectic of days because she knew that come the evening they would be together and the world would be shut out.

Roarke appeared happy too. At least the wastebasket in his office was spared the attentions of his foot these days. He had taken to spending most of his free time at her flat, only returning to his own apartment to pick up his mail. Sometimes they stayed in. More often they ate out or went to a show, but always when they came home they would make love.

Ginny was getting used to falling asleep in his arms, and waking to the gentle touch of his lips and hands in the morning. Like now. She had been awake for some time but she was pretending to be asleep for she loved the feel of his hands caressing her. He was so gentle, yet he could stir the embers inside her to life in no time at all. They lay moulded together spoon fashion, and she could feel his arousal pushing against her. It was becoming increasingly difficult to lie still, for as her body responded she wanted to move under his touch and purr like a cat.

'I know you're awake,' Roarke murmured in her ear before nibbling at her earlobe.

Released from the need for pretence, Ginny sighed ruefully and wriggled round to face him. 'Hi, do I know you?' she charged teasingly.

'Very well, if my memory serves me right,' he returned sardonically, running his hand over the curve of her hip and thigh. 'Um, this feels awfully familiar to me,' he added, grinning wolfishly.

Ginny shivered in response as a wave of tingles spread over her skin. 'And remind me just what it is you do,' she went on, tracing a finger down the line of his nose and round his lips.

'Oh, things like…this,' he told her with a wicked glint in his eye and trailed his hand to her breast, cupping it and circling her hardening nipple with his thumb.

Ginny sighed pleasurably. 'Ah, yes, now I remember you. We work together,' she declared, lowering her own hand to his chest and finding a flat male nipple nestling amongst the silky hairs.

'That's right.' Roarke nodded. 'It's always better when two people work together. It increases the pleasure.'

Her green eyes flirted with him. 'Is that so?'

'Want me to prove it to you?'

'I thought you'd never ask!' She laughed huskily. 'What do you want me to do?'

Laughing softly, Roarke eased her over on to her back and flung back the bedcovers. 'Nothing. All you have to do is lie there and take notes,' he told her against the tender skin of her neck. With infinite care he began to trace a wandering path over her body with lips and hands.

Biting her lip as a wave of pleasure washed over her, Ginny had to clear her throat to speak. 'Will you be asking questions later?' she asked, her laugh turning into a moan as he traversed the peaks of her breasts, leaving havoc in his wake.

Roarke paused in his roving somewhere around her navel and glanced up. 'The test will be a practical one. You have to repeat what you learn here. Points will be added for inventiveness,' he added as he returned to his ministrations.

She laughed, but when his hands parted her thighs and he sought the core of her with ravishing strokes of his tongue, amusement turned to gasping breaths and low moans of pleasure. With consummate ease he toppled her over the edge into a climax that appeased her immediate need, yet ultimately left her wanting more.

Roarke came up beside her, grinning wickedly. 'Do you understand what you have to do?' he asked teasingly, and Ginny sat up, eyes promising retribution.

'Let me see, we start here...' She trailed her fingers low across his stomach, and he jerked under her touch, taken by surprise. Smiling to herself, Ginny came up on her knees. 'No, no, that wasn't it.' She tutted. 'What about...?' Her hand closed around the velvety length of his manhood and squeezed gently.

'Hell's teeth!' Roarke exclaimed, coming up on his elbows, hot flags of colour staining his cheeks.

Instantly, Ginny was there, easing him back down. 'Take it easy. I'll get it right this time,' she promised, grinning devilishly, which made him groan and throw his arm over his eyes.

'You're nothing but a damned tease, Ginny Harte,' he told her tautly.

Ginny ran her hands over his chest, teasing the nipples into hardened nubs. 'I forgot to take notes—sorry. Something distracted me. Now, tell me how this feels.' Before he could guess what she was about, she was sitting astride his hips and had taken him inside her.

Roarke removed his arm and lay watching her, breathing raggedly. 'Feels good,' he murmured thickly.

'And this?' She moved, biting her lip as pleasure began to mount inside her.

'O—oh, yes,' he agreed through clenched teeth.

Her eyes met and held his as she continued to move seductively. It was incredibly arousing to entice him this way, but the need for satisfaction was growing inside her.

'Let go,' Roarke urged gruffly, and with a gasp she abandoned the fight for self-control and instead drove on towards the goal her body craved. Roarke's hands fastened on her hips as she flung her head back in an agony of pleasure, and he matched her rhythm. It was a wild, frantic ride, and minutes later they climaxed together with mingled cries.

Collapsing on top of him, Ginny closed her eyes and waited for her pulse to stop galloping. Finally she had enough breath to speak.

'It just keeps getting better and better, doesn't it?'

Roarke ran his hands caressingly up and down her back. 'Guess we must be doing something right.'

Sighing, she raised her hand and flicked her hair back out of her eyes. 'Was that inventive enough for you?'

'You can say that again. I don't know how I'm supposed to get up and go to work now.'

She knew how he felt, but the remark brought something else to mind. 'They're talking about us at the office, you know.'

'There's nothing new in that. They always talked about us,' Roarke was quick to point out.

'Yes, but now they're talking about us because we're not arguing. Do you think they suspect?'

'Probably.' Roarke used a finger to tease away hair that had stuck to her cheek. 'Do you mind them suspecting?'

'No,' she said with a shake of her head. It wasn't the

suspecting that bothered her, it was the knowledge that the staff would now be speculating on how long it would last, and how she would deal with the end of it. Something she didn't know herself and, frankly, didn't want to think about.

Sensing something was wrong, Roarke frowned. 'But?'

Easing herself away from him and sitting up, Ginny grimaced. 'It's nothing really. I simply realised that if they do suspect we're having an affair, they'll also be betting on how long it lasts. Your track record isn't good,' she reminded him dryly, making light of it though she wasn't that amused really. Whilst their attraction showed no signs of waning, she could not ignore the fact that the longer the affair lasted, the closer they came to the end. A prospect that was far from pleasant, though she wasn't ready to ask herself why.

Roarke sat up too. 'I'm sorry it's bothering you. Do you want me to put a stop to it?'

Ginny shook her head and slid off the bed, reaching for her robe and slipping it on. 'You can't stop them wondering. It's human nature.'

'Maybe not. But I don't like the idea of people gossiping about your private life.'

She laughed wryly. 'The only way to stop them is to end the affair. Is that what you want?'

'You know damn well it isn't,' Roarke growled, eyes gleaming wickedly. 'I don't know what makes you so different, but I can't get enough of you. There's no way I'm letting you go.'

It did her spirits a power of good to hear that, for she wasn't ready to end it, either. 'So we just let the gossips get on with it?'

'We're news now, but it will pass the minute something better comes along.'

He was right, of course, but as she showered a little while later she couldn't help remembering, and knowing that if they were news now one day she would be old news. It was a thought that tightened invisible fingers about her heart.

Ginny was busy working on a colour scheme for one of their small hotels, which was due to be redecorated in the off season, when Roarke let himself into her office via the connecting door. Glancing up, she smiled a welcome, then glanced at her watch.

'Hi. I thought you had a lunch appointment,' she reminded him, at the same time angling her head up to receive the kiss he deposited on her lips.

'I have,' he confirmed, perching himself on a corner of her desk. 'I just got off the phone from talking to Caroline.'

'They're back from their honeymoon at last? How are they?'

Roarke grinned. 'They're fine. They've been back a fortnight, apparently.'

Her brows rose. 'Two weeks? Where have they been hiding themselves?'

'In the house they've bought in Surrey. They've already entertained your parents, and my mother. Now it's our turn. We've been invited to dinner tonight,' Roarke informed her, and her smile faded to a wary look.

'Does James know?' Her last meeting with her brother had been less than comfortable.

'Um-hum. Apparently he's relaxed a lot. He even argued with your father during their visit.'

'James did?' Ginny couldn't have been more surprised. Her brother had had the stuffing knocked out of him by their father's strictness many years ago. That he would argue with him was tantamount to treason. 'I can't believe it. The Brigadier must have gone ballistic!'

Roarke rubbed the side of his nose judiciously. 'He wasn't too amused.'

Ginny started to laugh. 'Oh, I wish I could have seen that,' she said, wiping a tear from her eye. 'She didn't happen to say anything about Lucy?'

Ginny had been expecting her sister to turn up at her door ever since she had returned from Switzerland, but there had been no sign of her. Though she knew Lucy would come to no harm, she guessed that their father had been keeping an eagle eye on her, making it difficult for her to get away.

'No, she didn't. You'll have to ask her tonight. Are you worried about your sister?' Roarke asked in concern, and Ginny sighed, tapping her fingers on the desktop.

'No more than usual. I just wish she was here and not there.'

Roarke laid a reassuring hand on her shoulder. 'Lucy looked the resourceful type to me. She'll come when the time is right. Only she will know that.'

'You're right. It's the mother hen in me. I want her where I can look out for her,' Ginny replied wryly, then frowned as the rising sounds of a commotion in the outer office had them both turning and staring at the door.

'What on earth...?' Roarke muttered, but before he could make a move to go and investigate, the door was thrown open and Jenna stood in the doorway. 'Jenna?' he exclaimed in surprise, rising to his feet.

'Don't you Jenna me, you snake in the grass!' his stepmother declared in a loud voice. She took several not-quite-steady steps towards Ginny's desk, and it didn't take a genius to realise she had been drinking. It was by closing the distance between them that the woman finally recognised who Roarke was with. A sneer slid across her face. 'Well, well, well. If it isn't your little bedmate!' she exclaimed, and Ginny's heart sank as she saw the group of people huddled in the doorway. Judging from the looks on their faces, they had heard every damning word.

Roarke appreciated the situation too, and he waved the goggle-eyed group away. They went reluctantly, closing the door behind them. Only then did he turn his attention to the other woman.

'What are you doing here, Jenna?' he demanded to know in a voice that dripped ice.

'I came to tell you what I think of you, you rat! I suppose you're proud of yourselves, aren't you? You and this little tramp!' She waved a hand in Ginny's direction.

Frozen to her seat, Ginny was looking from one to the other like a spectator at a tennis match, but the thunderous expression on Roarke's face when he heard that made her catch her breath.

'Say what you like about me, Jenna, but don't even think of insulting Ginny in front of me. Believe me, you won't like what would happen next!' he told her in a voice so full of dislike the other woman must have felt it despite her condition.

'So that's the way the wind blows, is it? My, you must have got it bad to rush to her defence this way.' She laughed scornfully.

'My feelings for Ginny are none of your business.'

'What's she got that I haven't?' Jenna wanted to know.

Roarke folded his arms and looked at her stonily. 'Integrity, for one thing. The ability to care about other people. And she doesn't see dollar signs when she looks at a man. Will that do?'

Jenna shot him a vicious look. 'All I wanted was a little fun, you sanctimonious hypocrite. What was so wrong with that?'

'You were married to my father, but I take it from your presence here that's about to change.'

'He's divorcing me, the rat! And it was her fault.' She stabbed a finger towards Ginny.

That brought Ginny to her feet. 'I did nothing, Mrs Adams,' she denied calmly. 'It was all your own work.'

Jenna glared at her. 'You said something to him. I know you did!'

Ginny shook her head. 'I said nothing. I admit I was going to, but as it turned out I didn't have to. Lewis had already seen through you.'

The other woman seethed with anger, and it took away any trace of her beauty. 'You think you're so smart, don't you? Well, Roarke may have the hots for you, darling, but he'll never marry you. He's all screwed up inside when it comes to love and marriage. So don't think you've got it made! You'll never keep him.'

Ginny looked at her coldly. 'I think you should go now, Mrs Adams.'

Jenna slayed them with a withering look. 'Don't worry, I'm leaving. The sooner I'm free of this lousy family, the better! There are other fish in the sea, and I'm going fishing!' she exclaimed, and flung herself out of the office with another crash of the door.

After a stunned moment when neither of them moved, Roarke crossed the room and shut the door after her. Letting out his breath in a silent whistle, he ran a hand through his hair. 'Jenna always did know how to make an entrance *and* an exit. Let's hope we've seen the last of her,' he declared feelingly. 'I'm sorry for the way she spoke to you.'

Ginny smiled faintly. 'That's OK. I have broad shoulders.'

Roarke grimaced. 'You're going to need them. If the staff didn't know about us before, they know now.'

She pulled a similarly wry face. 'So much for secrecy, then.' By now the office grapevine would have spread the news far and wide. 'What brought her here?'

'The desire to hurt me. She thinks if she can break us up, justice will have been done,' Roarke explained with a shake of his head.

Ginny frowned. 'But there's nothing to break up. We aren't in love with each other,' she added, when he looked a query. 'We're just…'

He eyed her with curiosity, amusement dancing in his eyes. 'Just?'

She narrowed her eyes at him. 'You know what I mean. We don't have that kind of relationship.'

Roarke pursed his lips as he considered that. 'No, we don't. It's just good old-fashioned sex,' he agreed at last.

She nodded, although the description didn't sit well. However, there was no denying the truth. Put plainly, it was just sex. 'Anyway, I'm not expecting a proposal.'

'That's comforting,' he rejoined sardonically, and she frowned at him.

'I just wanted you to know…'

'That ours is not a love affair. I got the message.'

Ginny blinked at his odd behaviour. 'Are you feeling all right?'

He laughed wryly. 'To tell you the truth, I'm not quite

sure. Look, I'm late for that meeting. Let's just forget about Jenna, OK?'

Blowing her a kiss, Roarke vanished back into his office and Ginny slumped into her seat, running over the last half-hour in her mind. Jenna's sudden appearance had certainly created a stir. The cat was out of the bag now, but she found she wasn't worried about that. What she did find uncomfortable was Roarke's description of their relationship.

True, they enjoyed great sex, but that wasn't all of it. She enjoyed being with him, and it was amazing how much they had in common. So it wasn't just sex. On the other hand, she didn't know what word to use to accurately describe it. It certainly wasn't love! She didn't love Roarke. She wanted him, but that wasn't love. So it had to be sex, and yet... It just didn't sit right, that was all.

With an irritable sigh, Ginny forced herself to forget about it. It was just words, after all. Semantics. It was what it was and that was that. There. Finished. She reached for the colour charts she had been studying before Jenna's arrival and gave them her total concentration. If her thoughts wandered from time to time, she dragged them back into line with grim determination.

Later that evening, Ginny sat beside Roarke in his car, her stomach churning with nerves. This dinner with Caroline and James was going to be very important and she hoped she didn't do or say anything to mess it up. She glanced across at Roarke, but he was concentrating on the road. He had been strangely quiet since he returned from his lunch appointment, almost introspective, and that added to her sense of disquiet. What was he thinking? It could be business, but generally he left that behind when they left the office. Tonight, however, his thoughts were elsewhere, and she couldn't help thinking it had something to do with Jenna's visit.

Having crossed the Thames, they were now driving through a leafy suburb, and Roarke turned into a road lined with large detached houses set back from the road. Eventually he steered the car through a pair of wrought-iron gates on to a driveway and parked the car before the house.

'Very nice,' he declared as he came round to open the door for her. 'At a guess, I would say it was a wedding present from our mother.'

'The Brigadier would have been impressed,' Ginny observed dryly. A sound behind them made them glance round, to see the gates gliding shut. She laughed. 'No uninvited guests. Good idea.' There could be a problem with crime here, but Ginny rather thought the gates would have been Caroline's idea.

Roarke smiled as they walked to the door. 'I told you Caroline was a determined woman.'

'Not only determined,' his sister declared from the door where she stood waiting, having anticipated them. 'But clever, too.' She stood back with a smile to allow them to step inside. 'I'm so happy to see you again, Ginny,' she said, giving Ginny a hug. 'Has Roarke been behaving himself?' she asked, kissing her brother fondly on the cheek.

'Mostly,' Ginny returned, handing her evening jacket to the waiting housekeeper.

'Good. I'm so glad the two of you are still together. Of course, I was pretty sure you would be,' she added, with a twinkle in her eye.

Ginny exchanged an amused look with Roarke, who raised his shoulders in a helpless shrug.

'Where's James?' she asked. The fact that he wasn't at the door didn't bode well.

Caroline's response surprised her. 'He's in the drawing room mixing Martinis. He's nervous.'

'He is?' That was a first! James had always seemed so sure of himself.

Roarke's sister shepherded them towards a doorway. 'He thinks you might be angry with him. He wasn't very nice to you at the wedding,' she explained.

'He wasn't, but that made me sad, not angry,' Ginny replied wistfully.

The drawing room was large and designed for comfort. James was standing at a sideboard pouring liquid from a mixer into four glasses. He glanced round as they walked in, set the mixer aside and visibly braced himself with a deep breath before coming to join his wife.

'Hello, Roarke.' He shook his brother-in-law's hand, then looked at his sister warily. 'Ginny.'

Ginny searched his eyes, seeing some unease there, but the nervous tension that had always been with him when their father was around had vanished. As Caroline had said all those weeks ago, getting him away from his father would do him a world of good, and Ginny could see that it had. Consequently, she smiled at him and held out her hand.

'Hello, James,' she said huskily, then held her breath as he hesitated. However, it was only for a moment, and then he was squeezing her hand tightly.

'Good of you to come,' James added gruffly, clearing his throat. 'I wasn't sure you would.'

His uncertainty brought moisture to her eyes, and she

shook her head then laughed, overwhelmed by a mixture of emotions. 'You know me better than that. You're my brother and I love you.'

James's throat worked madly, and he shot a glance at his wife, who nodded encouragingly from the sidelines. 'I said some pretty rotten things to you.'

Ginny sighed, unable to deny it. 'Yes, you did. But I understood why, James. I've always understood. All I care about now is that I can see you and talk to you. You don't have to tell our father anything about it. Let's leave him and the past out of it and just be friends. Can you do that? Will you do that?'

'It's what I would like, if you can forgive me,' her brother responded stiffly, and without having to think about it Ginny slipped her arms about his neck and hugged him, feeling her heart swell as, after a short pause, he hugged her back.

'There's nothing to forgive. Nothing,' she told him, stepping back, and then Caroline stepped in and hugged them all, and the tears were replaced by laughter.

As she watched Caroline shoo James off to fetch the drinks, Ginny felt Roarke take her hand and squeeze it. She glanced up at him.

'OK?' he asked simply, and when she nodded he bent and pressed a swift kiss to her lips.

It seemed to Ginny, as she took the glass James handed her and they toasted each other, that life couldn't get any better.

From then on the evening buzzed with laughter. Ginny couldn't remember her brother ever being so relaxed, and she had quite forgotten that he had a wacky sense of humour. She couldn't have said what they ate for dinner, though it tasted wonderful. She was too busy watching and listening. The banter between Roarke and his sister showed them how family life should be, and Ginny was determined that that was how it would be once Lucy broke away.

She enjoyed watching James relax, and caught sight of the boy he had been, but mostly she watched Roarke. She sat back, fascinated by the play of emotions over his face as he said something serious or told a joke. Somehow, she just couldn't seem to take her eyes off him, and when he glanced her way and quirked a questioning eyebrow to check that she was all right, she smiled, feeling a warm sense of well-being swell up inside her. She was happy, and happiness had been in short supply all of her life. Which was why she hugged the feeling to her, for it was precious beyond words.

Eventually a lull fell as they exchanged the wine for coffee, and it was during the lull that Caroline set the cat among the pigeons.

'So,' she said, looking from her brother to Ginny. 'When are you two getting engaged?'

Ginny blinked and almost choked on her after-dinner mint. Roarke had gone still, his cup halfway to his lips.

'What?' they asked in unison, casting cautionary glances at each other, which Caroline found highly amusing.

'Oh, come on,' she chided. 'I can't recall ever seeing you so happy, Roarke. It must be love!'

Roarke set his cup down with a sharp tap of china on china. 'I'm not in love,' he said bluntly, and Ginny caught her breath sharply as she was struck by an unexpected shaft of pain. 'Neither of us are.' He looked to Ginny for confirmation, and she turned to his sister.

'We don't have that kind of relationship.' She repeated

the phrase she had used only hours before. It sounded lame now.

'Fiddlesticks!' Caroline exclaimed. 'Are you both ostriches? What kind of relationship do you think you have?'

James put his hand on his wife's arm. 'Er, Caro, I don't think this is the right time,' he warned awkwardly.

She frowned at him. 'But it's obvious!'

He smiled at Ginny and Roarke, then held his wife's gaze pointedly. 'Not to them, darling.'

Caroline looked confused. 'But...' She frowned at her brother. 'You're...not...in love?'

'No.'

Once again they spoke together.

The other woman's shoulders slumped and she shook her head. 'Well, OK, if you say you're not, you're not. Who am I to argue?'

'Surely we should know?' Ginny put in, trying to ease the uncomfortable moment, and Caroline smiled ruefully.

'Of course you should, Ginny. Forget I ever mentioned it,' she ordered, smiling at everyone. 'Now, who wants a brandy to go with their coffee?'

So the awkward moment was glossed over, and the remainder of the evening passed without anything else untoward happening. However, as they drove home, Ginny couldn't help thinking about it.

'It's funny that your sister should think we're in love,' she remarked. 'What made her think that?'

'Being in the happy state herself, no doubt,' Roarke returned sardonically, then spared her a glance. 'You don't love me, do you?'

Ginny turned startled eyes his way. 'I think I'd know. You don't?'

'You know my feelings on the subject. Love is for the birds.'

'So it's still sex, then?' She sought confirmation.

'Just sex,' he agreed, and they fell silent.

Ginny stared out into the darkness and saw her own reflection. It seemed to be asking a question. If this was just sex, why did she suddenly feel so empty inside? Neither she nor her reflection had an answer.

CHAPTER TEN

ABOUT ten days later Ginny stirred in the night, and knew instantly that she was alone in the bed. Running a hand over the sheets, she found they were cool, and knew that Roarke had been gone some time. Sliding from the bed, she slipped on her robe and went in search of him. He had been acting a little strangely ever since they had had dinner with Caroline and James, and now finding him out of bed like this gave her a vague feeling of disquiet.

She almost didn't see him. Roarke was sitting on the sofa in the dark, his feet propped up on the coffee table. She stood and watched him in silence, unable to dispel the feeling that he was a million miles away instead of just a few feet.

'What are you doing here in the dark?' she asked quietly, and his head turned towards her.

'Just sitting and thinking. I thought you were asleep.'

She padded into the room. 'Something woke me, and I discovered you were gone. Can't you sleep? Is something bothering you?'

Roarke held out a hand to her, and Ginny took it, allowing herself to be pulled down on to the sofa beside him. She tucked her feet under her and rested herself against him. The closeness should have helped but, contrarily, it didn't quite. She still had the feeling something was wrong, but couldn't put a finger on it.

'I'm going to New York tomorrow morning,' he said into the darkness.

Ginny frowned, for there was nothing scheduled or she

would have known about it. 'You are? Has something happened?' she asked in all seriousness, and was surprised to hear Roarke laugh wryly.

'You could say that. There are some…people I have to see,' he added, and she didn't miss the faint hesitation.

People? That was an odd way of putting it. 'You're making it sound very mysterious.'

'Am I? Well, it isn't. It's just something I have to do. For Grandfather,' he explained, and Ginny felt a sense of relief totally out of proportion to the situation, which showed how uneasy she had been feeling lately.

'Oh, I see. Family business. Ah, well, if he needs you, he needs you, but I'll miss you,' she declared, touching a hand to his chest.

'I'll miss you, too,' he responded, dropping a kiss on her head.

A lump lodged itself in her throat as she started to miss him already. 'How long will you be gone?'

Roarke ran his hand gently up and down her arm. 'I really have no idea, but not too long, I hope.'

'Do you want me to pack for you?' she offered helpfully, but he shook his head.

'No. I'll pop into my apartment on the way to the airport and collect some fresh things from there.'

Ginny sighed heavily. 'I don't suppose you can pack me in your suitcase and take me with you?' she joked, though if he had asked she would have gone with him in a trice.

He laughed huskily. 'Much as I would like to have you with me, this is something I have to do alone.'

'There's nothing I can do to change your mind?' she asked, running her hand over his chest and slipping it inside the towelling robe he was wearing.

Roarke's free hand came up and stopped her roving one

in its tracks. 'There's plenty you could do, but it won't make me change my mind, sweetheart.'

She hadn't supposed it would, but it was worth a try. 'Will you ring me? Let me know how things are going on?'

Roarke raised the hand he held captive to his lips and pressed a kiss to her palm. 'Every day, and that's a promise.'

As satisfied as she could be with the situation, Ginny eased herself away from him and stood up. 'Come back to bed, then, and let me give you something to remember whilst you're away,' she suggested huskily, and she saw his teeth flash in the darkness as he grinned and stood up.

'There might be some men who could ignore an offer like that, but I'm not one of them, thank God,' he declared, sweeping her up into his arms and striding back to the bedroom.

Maybe it was knowing that they would be apart for some time that gave their lovemaking a degree of urgency which made it impossible for either of them to hold back. From the first touch they wanted each other with a hunger and need that would not be denied, and the result was white-hot passion. Limbs tangled, bodies grew slick with sweat, and their moans of almost unbearable pleasure led on to a climax that left them so satiated they fell asleep in each other's arms.

Roarke had showered and was already eating breakfast when she woke next morning. Memories of the night before brought a smile to her lips as she showered and dressed, then joined him in her tiny kitchen.

Their eyes met and a silent message passed, though neither mentioned the passion they had shared. They remembered, and that was enough.

'What time's your flight?' she asked, nibbling at a piece

of toast whilst watching him wash his breakfast things and set them on the drainer.

'Eleven. I'll have time to run you to work, then go on to my apartment,' Roarke informed her after glancing at his watch.

'You'll be exhausted. You didn't get a lot of sleep last night,' she commiserated with him, though her eyes twinkled flirtatiously.

He grinned ruefully. 'Never mind. I can catch up on lost sleep during the flight.'

Ginny pulled a face. 'I wish you weren't going.'

Rounding the table, he tipped her chin up and kissed her deeply. 'It's important I do this. I'll tell you all about it when I get back. Now, get a move on or we'll both be late.'

She rose, finishing off her toast and taking a last sip of coffee before following him. 'I'll have to complain to my boss about you.'

Roarke laughed. 'Think it will do you any good?' Collecting his briefcase, he waited by the door.

'We—ell, I do have some influence with him. I have a trick or two up my sleeve,' she teased, slipping on the jacket of her suit and gathering up her bag.

He held the door for her to precede him out. 'Save them till I get back, then we'll try them out and see how effective they'll be,' he suggested, and Ginny floated down the stairs with a sigh of contentment.

Roarke was as good as his word and telephoned her each evening, just when he knew she would be in bed. The sound of his voice kept her spirits up, but she missed him terribly. More than she thought she could possibly miss anyone. The days dragged by, but the nights were the worst. She missed his presence in the bed beside her.

Roarke had become a vital part of her life without her even realising it was happening. She felt as if a part of herself was missing, and couldn't wait for him to come back.

Working helped, and she buried herself in it so as not to daydream about what Roarke might be doing. A few days into his trip, she was busily working out a timetable for some renovation work when Roarke's grandfather called.

'Where's that grandson of mine got to?' Stephen Adams's voice demanded down the telephone line. 'His secretary tells me he's abroad.'

Naturally, Ginny blinked, surprised by the question. He had to know where Roarke was. He had sent him there. She couldn't help wondering if his memory was getting a little rusty with age. 'He's in New York, Mr Adams,' she reminded him politely, aiming to jog his memory. His response startled her.

'What's he doing there?' the elderly gentleman asked in astonishment.

She frowned at the receiver, more than a little alarmed by this depth of forgetfulness. 'He's doing whatever it was you sent him to do, Mr Adams,' she enlarged, unable to help more because she was in the dark too.

'My dear Ginny, I may be old but I am not yet senile. I never sent Roarke to New York. Why would I do that? He's supposed to be playing golf with me tomorrow,' Stephen Adams challenged, sounding amused, but Ginny froze, her stomach knotting.

What was going on here? She wasn't mistaken about what Roarke had said, and yet his grandfather was saying he knew nothing about it. Licking her lips, she sought confirmation. 'Roarke told me he had something to do for you. Are you saying that's not the case?'

'I most certainly am, young Ginny,' Roarke's grand-father confirmed, and she closed her eyes as she realised he had lied to her.

Ginny pressed her fingers to where an ache had started up between her eyes. 'I'm sorry, I must have misunder-stood what he said,' she apologised. 'Roarke is in New York, though.' At least she thought he was ringing from America. For all she knew, he could be in Timbuktu. It gave her a queasy feeling to realise she had no real idea where he was.

'When's he coming back?'

'I don't know when he's due back. He couldn't say.' Couldn't or wouldn't?

Stephen Adams harrumphed down the line, not best pleased. 'I'll have something to say to that young man when he gets back. This is our Saturday grudge match. We haven't missed one in ages.'

Ginny sympathised and they exchanged a few more words, then Stephen Adams rang off and Ginny sank back into her chair, feeling chilled to the bone.

What was going on? She knew full well what Roarke had said, and she would have gone on believing it if his grandfather hadn't called. Why had Roarke found it nec-essary to lie to her? It hurt incredibly to know that he had. The only answer she could come up with was that he didn't want her to know what he was doing. That made her angry as well. He could have just told her it was private. He hadn't had to lie like that. Anger fuelled by hurt seethed in her for the rest of the day. By the time she headed home she had made up her mind that he was going to have some explaining to do that night.

That evening she was a bundle of nervous energy as she waited for the telephone to ring. Unable to sit still, she prowled around her flat like a big cat in a cage. When the call finally came, she took a deep breath and lifted the receiver.

'Hello?'

'Ginny?' Roarke queried in some surprise. 'Are you all right?' Obviously, though she had tried to sound normal, he must have picked something up. In which case, she wasn't going to put on a pretence of being happy when she was far from it.

Folding her arm across her waist, Ginny paced away as far as the flex would allow. 'Do I sound OK?' she challenged, that seething mix of anger and hurt growing inside her.

There was a brief pause before Roarke answered. 'You sound...odd.'

Her eyes narrowed. 'That's funny. I thought I sounded angry,' she retorted, pacing back to the sofa.

'What's wrong, Ginny?' Roarke asked shortly, and she smiled to herself, choosing to ignore the question.

'How's New York?' she asked instead, with false brightness.

'New York is fine. What's wrong?' His tone was more abrupt, and she could sense his growing unease.

'You are *in* New York, aren't you?' she queried next, and felt the tension coming down the line to her.

Roarke took a steadying breath. 'I told you I was. Ginny...' he began patiently but she interrupted him.

'Your grandfather called today,' she informed him tersely, and the silence which followed the words was palpably fraught. 'He was just checking that your golf match was still on for tomorrow. It was careless of you to forget about that when you lied to me.'

'I didn't lie to you, Ginny,' Roarke said carefully, and she could sense his frustration that this conversation was taking place over the phone and not where he could see her.

Ginny laughed harshly. 'Of course you didn't lie, you were just being economical with the truth! That's what they say these days, isn't it?'

'This is impossible!' he declared in exasperation. 'I can't explain to you over the phone.'

'Just tell me why you had to lie,' she commanded, feeling the sting of angry tears behind her eyes.

'I lied because I couldn't tell you the truth.'

'Gee whizz, Roarke, I never would have worked that out for myself!' she shot back scathingly. What kind of an answer was that to give an angry woman?

'Sweetheart, I can't explain over the phone, it's too complicated. Will you please stop getting upset?' he urged down the line.

A single tear trailed hotly down her cheek and she brushed it away. 'I'm not upset. I'm furious!' she corrected, and again there was a pregnant silence.

'You feel that strongly about it, do you?' Roarke asked searchingly.

'I want to murder you!' she added.

'Why?' he asked simply.

'Why what?' Ginny launched back, prowling to the window.

'Why are you furious, Ginny?' Roarke spelt it out for her. There was an expectant edge to his voice, as if the answer was really important to him.

She held the receiver away from her ear for a moment and glared at it. 'Why am I furious? You lied to me, that's why!'

'Have you any idea what you sound like?' Roarke asked in the wake of her explosion, and to Ginny he almost sounded amused. It had the effect of stoking the angry fire inside her.

'I don't care what I sound like!' she snapped, and he laughed. He actually had the gall to laugh.

'Well, I do care, and to me you sound like a woman who feels she's been betrayed,' Roarke told her with a certain amount of satisfaction.

Adding that to everything else, it was no wonder Ginny's temper hit the roof. 'You're darn right I feel betrayed! I thought I could trust you. You had no right to lie to me for whatever reason! There are no good reasons for doing what you did! It hurt, damn it!'

'Why?' he asked softly.

'Because I love you, you horrible man!' she exclaimed wrathfully, then went into total shock when she realised what she had said. Her hand went to her mouth as she stared at the receiver as if it were a snake. 'Oh, God!' she whispered, then slammed the receiver back down.

Almost immediately, it rang again but, knowing who it must be, Ginny jiggled the receiver to cut off the call and then set it down beside the phone. She sank slowly on to the sofa, pressing her hands to scalding cheeks. What had she done? How on earth could she have just told Roarke she loved him?

The answer was simple. She had said it because it was the truth. She had fallen in love with him. Only being in love with him would explain why she felt betrayed by his lying to her. Having finally admitted it, she now realised she had loved him for a long time. Maybe even from the beginning.

As she sat there, the shock began to subside and she fully appreciated the discovery she had made. She loved Roarke Adams with a depth and breadth she hadn't thought possible. He was everything she wanted, she told herself, then her shoulders slumped as she grimaced. He was also the one person she couldn't have. Because Roarke didn't want to love or be loved. He had been more than clear about it.

And, just minutes ago, she had told him what he least wanted to hear. She hadn't meant to. He had made her so angry, the words had just slipped out. She groaned helplessly. If only she hadn't said it. They could have gone on the way they were, with her being the only one who knew, but now… He wouldn't like it.

What was she going to do if he wanted to end the relationship? What *could* she do? She uttered another heartfelt groan. Lord, what a fool she was. Trust her to deal a knockout blow to the one thing that really mattered in her life! It was over. It had to be. They wanted different things from life.

Ginny went from the heights of elation in realising how much she loved him, to plumb the depths of defeat. She called herself all the names she could think of for being so stupid, but in the end it changed nothing. She loved him, he wouldn't love her…and no doubt when he came back he would tell her it was all over. Well, she wasn't going to weep all over him. She had her pride. It wasn't his fault she had fallen in love with him. She'd managed to make that mistake all on her own.

Sighing, she reached out and replaced the receiver back on its rest. If he rang she would speak to him. After all, she had already made a big enough fool of herself. What else could she do?

Roarke didn't ring, but half an hour later the front doorbell startled her. It was getting late, close to midnight, and Ginny took care to look through the peephole before considering opening the door. The figure she saw standing in

the fisheye had her fumbling with the locks and throwing
the door wide.

'Lucy!' she exclaimed in delight. 'I'd almost given up
on you!' she added, picking up the case sitting by the
door, and pulling her sister inside.

'I had to wait until Dad dropped his guard,' Lucy explained as the sisters hugged each other. 'I'm sorry I arrived so late, but it took longer than I expected.'

'You didn't walk here at this time of night, did you?'
Ginny gasped, shuddering at the idea. No street was really
safe these days.

Lucy shook her head. 'No. Peter borrowed a friend's
car and dropped me off. I thought you might have been
in bed, but then we saw the light on.'

Ginny wasn't about to go into why she was still up. It
was bad enough knowing the reason herself, let alone
spreading it around. 'Have you eaten? Can I make you
something? A sandwich? How about a cup of tea or coffee?'

'I'm fine, really,' Lucy refused with a laugh. 'We had
something a little while ago. Are you sure it's OK for me
to be here?'

'Of course it is. I already made up the spare bed. Come
and see.' Ginny led the way to the box-like room that
passed as the second bedroom. It was small but cosy, with
a view over some gardens. 'You can stay here as long as
you like.'

Lucy retrieved her case from the hallway and laid it on
the bed before looking at her sister with serious eyes.
'You're sure this is OK with Roarke? Where is he?'

Ginny felt faint colour wash into her cheeks at the question. 'Er, he's in New York at the moment, but I know
he'll be glad you're here.'

'I'd hate to be a gooseberry,' her sister teased, then

tried to stifle a big yawn. 'I'm sorry. I really wanted to sit and have a long chat with you, but now I'm here I can barely keep my eyes open.'

'Don't worry. We'll talk in the morning. We've got plenty of time now. The bathroom's across the hall, and my room is the next door along. Make yourself at home,' Ginny told her as she walked to the door. 'Help yourself to anything in the kitchen, and you know where I am if you need me.' She turned to leave, but hesitated and glanced back over her shoulder. 'It's wonderful to have you here at last, Lucy.'

'I'm glad to be here,' Lucy responded thickly and Ginny closed the door before her sister could see the tears in her eyes.

Life was strange. If something had gone badly wrong today, then something else had gone wonderfully right to balance it out. Feeling happier than she had been an hour ago, Ginny headed for her bed.

She was jolted awake the next morning by someone thundering on her front door. Squinting at the clock, she saw it was after nine but, as she had slept only fitfully, Ginny was not best pleased. Scrambling from her bed, she grabbed up her robe and tied the belt around her waist as the ruckus continued.

'All right, all right!' she muttered as she stomped to the door.

Lucy appeared in the doorway of the other bedroom, looking mussed from sleep. 'Who is it?'

'Haven't a clue,' Ginny returned grouchily. 'Whoever they are, they're going to get the rough edge of my tongue!'

The banging continued. 'Open up!' a familiar voice ordered and Ginny stiffened, glancing at Lucy, who had frozen on the spot. They both knew who was on the other side of the door. 'Go in the bathroom and lock the door,' she ordered, and didn't move to unfasten the locks until her sister had scuttled across the hall and she had heard the key turn.

The second Ginny turned the latch, the door was thrust backwards, crashing against the wall and rebounding towards the man who strode into the flat, allowing nothing and no one to stand in his way.

'Where is she?' Sir Martin demanded to know, rounding on Ginny, who had followed in his wake.

Ginny folded her arms and prepared to do battle. 'Do you make a habit of bursting into other people's homes like this?'

Her father ignored the question. 'I'm here to take your sister home with me. Where is she?'

'How did you know where to find me?' Ginny wanted to know first. Her telephone number was ex-directory, so she wasn't in the book.

'I had someone do a background check on you. It was fascinating to discover you work for Adams. What did you do, sleep your way to the top?' Sir Martin looked down his nose at her, and Ginny gritted her teeth.

'I think you had better leave before I call the police,' she said coldly.

'I'm not leaving without Lucy.'

'You're certainly not leaving with her. She's eighteen and she's not answerable to anyone but herself,' Ginny countered.

'Hah! So she is here! I knew you would be responsible for poisoning her mind against me.'

'On the contrary, Sir Martin, you managed to alienate your family all by yourself,' Roarke's frosty voice declared from behind, and they both turned.

Ginny felt her cheeks turn pink as she faced him. The last words she had spoken to him had been stunners. 'Roarke!' She managed to croak out his name.

Smiling faintly, he strolled to her side and draped an arm around her shoulders. 'Hi,' he greeted her softly, and dropped a swift kiss on her surprised lips. Then he turned his attention back to her father. 'Lucy is staying here with us. You can leave as soon as you like. The door is open.'

'How dare you order me about?' Sir Martin spluttered.

'I dare because I won't let you hurt any of the people I care about,' Roarke told him bluntly.

'Lucy is my daughter…' Sir Martin started to bluster, but Roarke took a step towards him and he faltered to a stop.

'Ginny is your daughter, too, and look what you did to her. My God, you disgust me. You had something precious and you threw it away. Well, I found it and I intend to keep it, for I value Ginny far above anything you could possibly name,' he told the older man in a voice that shook with suppressed emotion.

'You're welcome to her. And if Lucy chooses to stay here, you're welcome to her, too,' Sir Martin snarled. Turning to go, he came face to face with his youngest daughter, who had come out of the bathroom at the sound of Roarke's voice. 'Well, are you coming?' he demanded, and Lucy stepped out of his way.

'I'm staying.'

'Then I wash my hands of the lot of you!' he declared scornfully. 'You're no children of mine!' He walked out without a backward glance and seconds later they heard the front door slam shut.

Lucy hurried across the room and hugged first Ginny and then Roarke. 'Thank you. Thank you both so much. You were marvellous,' she said huskily. Then, because she was young, her spirits lifted and she grinned at them. 'I can't believe it's over and he's gone. I think I'll go and ring Peter and tell him the good news.'

'You can use the phone in my room,' Ginny offered, smiling at her happy face.

'Thanks, I will,' her sister chirped, almost dancing across the room. However, she halted in the doorway and looked back. 'Did you mean what you said about Ginny?' she asked Roarke.

He smiled back at her. 'Every word.'

Lucy laughed. 'Then I'll stay out of the way for a while, shall I?'

'We'd be grateful,' he told her dryly, and she waved her fingers at them before disappearing.

The second she was gone Ginny, who had been stunned to hear him utter those words to her father, squared up to him.

'You shouldn't lie to Lucy. You couldn't possibly mean what you said,' she said sternly, and Roarke quirked an eyebrow at her.

'Why not?'

Ginny really wasn't in the mood for games. She just wanted him to get the bad news over with. 'Because we both know you don't...care about me.'

He smiled faintly. 'We do? I don't?'

Already agitated, she didn't care for him pushing her buttons one by one. 'Don't mess with me. You know I'm just the woman you...'

'Have great sex with?' he offered helpfully, and his grey eyes glittered with amusement and something else she couldn't put a name to.

Hot colour stained her cheeks at the blunt words, and she turned her back on him because emotional tears were stinging her eyes, making them sparkle like diamonds.

'OK, have your fun. I know I deserve it. I've ruined everything with what I said last night. If you hadn't made me so mad, it never would have popped out and surprised us both!'

'I'm glad it did. It was what I was aiming for, after all,' Roarke informed her matter-of-factly, and she spun round, her mouth dropping open.

'What?'

'I do love you, you know,' Roarke told her simply. 'I tried to tell you as much last night, but you hung up on me.'

Ginny searched his eyes, her heart lurching madly in her chest. She saw an earnestness there that seemed to suggest he meant it, but… 'You can't love me. You told me you don't intend to love anyone!' she exclaimed breathlessly.

'I know I did, and up until a few days ago I fully believed I meant it. Then something happened to change my mind,' he told her gently. 'I had to get away to check it out. *That* was why I went to New York. I couldn't tell you until I was certain, so I lied about the trip. My mind was so mixed up I forgot about Grandfather, though.'

Having spent a night of sheer misery, cursing her own foolishness, Ginny only slowly began to accept that the sky hadn't fallen in after all. On the contrary, a miracle had happened.

Her heart began to swell with unexpected joy. 'You really love me?' she asked in a voice thick with emotion.

The laughter faded from his eyes, and he looked down at her intently. 'I really do.'

Tears overflowed, but they were happy ones. It only took a step to bring her to him, and then she threw her arms about his neck and hugged him painfully close. 'Oh, God, I thought I'd ruined everything!' she exclaimed, and

Roarke framed her head with his hands and looked down at her.

'Instead your anger gave me hope. I nudged you into saying what I wanted to hear, but when I wanted to tell you how I felt, you cut me off. So I caught the first plane out in order to get to you and make it right. Have I made it right? Do you forgive me for deceiving you?'

Her smile was watery. 'It couldn't be righter. And of course I forgive you. How could I not, when I love you so much?'

'Then come and kiss me. I need it like a thirsty man needs water,' he growled.

It was a kiss like no other they had shared for, whilst passion hovered in the background, this kiss was a promise. A sealing of what they had just said in words. It transcended the physical, and yet left them with a sense of profound fulfilment.

'So, what made you change your mind about love?' Ginny asked some time later when Roarke had carried her to the sofa and stretched out on it with her in his arms.

'Caroline,' he replied, rubbing his cheek gently over her hair. 'She thought we were in love. She thought it was obvious. So I asked myself the question. Did I love you? The reply stunned me. I did.'

Ginny settled her hand over his heart, feeling it beating strongly. 'So why did you go to New York?'

'Because I had to be sure. I went to the place where I was bound to run into any number of attractive available women. Do you know what I found out? I wasn't interested in a single one of them. The highlight of my day was talking to you at night. It didn't take more than forty-eight hours to make me certain I didn't want anyone else.'

'It only took me ten minutes,' Ginny countered smugly. 'After I'd winkled the truth out of you!'

'That was a dastardly trick. Do you know how miserable I was, thinking I'd scored an own goal?' she charged aggrievedly.

Roarke laughed. 'I'll make it up to you.'

'The list is growing. You already said I could have anything I want for agreeing to help you out,' she reminded him.

'I did say that, didn't I? Have you decided what it's to be?'

Ginny smiled to herself as her finger traced lazy patterns over his shirt. 'I think what I would really like is a baby. Two, actually, to keep each other company. Then we could add to them as time goes by.'

Roarke laughed huskily. 'Don't you think we should get married first?'

She lifted herself enough to meet his eyes. 'Are you asking me?'

'Sounds like it,' he confirmed lazily.

'Then the answer is yes. However, it doesn't stop us working on the baby, does it?' she flirted with him, eyes gleaming suggestively.

Roarke groaned and settled her back down. 'You're shameless, do you know that? You only said it because Lucy's in your bedroom.'

Ginny laughed happily. 'She won't be long. Besides, we have time. All the time in the world.'

Which was just as well, for when Lucy came out of the bedroom some time later she found them wrapped in each other's arms, fast asleep.

The world's bestselling romance series.

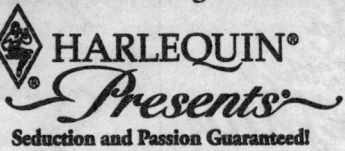

HARLEQUIN®
Presents

Seduction and Passion Guaranteed!

Coming soon...
To the rescue...armed with a ring!

Marriage is their mission!
Look out for more stories of
Modern-Day Knights...

Coming next month:
NATHAN'S CHILD
by Anne McAllister
#2333

Coming in August
AT THE SPANIARD'S PLEASURE
by Jacqueline Baird
#2337

Pick up a Harlequin Presents® novel and you will enter a world of spine-tingling passion and provocative, tantalizing romance!

Available wherever Harlequin books are sold.

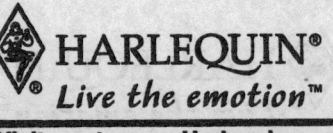

HARLEQUIN®
Live the emotion™

If you enjoyed what you just read,
then we've got an offer you can't resist!

Take 2 bestselling love stories FREE!

Plus get a FREE surprise gift!

Clip this page and mail it to Harlequin Reader Service®

IN U.S.A.
3010 Walden Ave.
P.O. Box 1867
Buffalo, N.Y. 14240-1867

IN CANADA
P.O. Box 609
Fort Erie, Ontario
L2A 5X3

YES! Please send me 2 free Harlequin Presents® novels and my free surprise gift. After receiving them, if I don't wish to receive anymore, I can return the shipping statement marked cancel. If I don't cancel, I will receive 6 brand-new novels every month, before they're available in stores! In the U.S.A., bill me at the bargain price of $3.57 plus 25¢ shipping & handling per book and applicable sales tax, if any*. In Canada, bill me at the bargain price of $4.24 plus 25¢ shipping & handling per book and applicable taxes**. That's the complete price and a savings of at least 10% off the cover prices—what a great deal! I understand that accepting the 2 free books and gift places me under no obligation ever to buy any books. I can always return a shipment and cancel at any time. Even if I never buy another book from Harlequin, the 2 free books and gift are mine to keep forever.

106 HDN DNTZ
306 HDN DNT2

Name	(PLEASE PRINT)	
Address	Apt.#	
City	State/Prov.	Zip/Postal Code

* Terms and prices subject to change without notice. Sales tax applicable in N.Y.
** Canadian residents will be charged applicable provincial taxes and GST.
All orders subject to approval. Offer limited to one per household and not valid to current Harlequin Presents® subscribers.
® are registered trademarks of Harlequin Enterprises Limited.

PRES02   ©2001 Harlequin Enterprises Limited

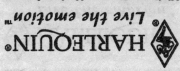

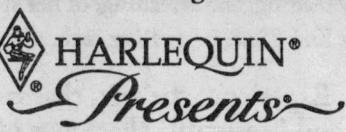

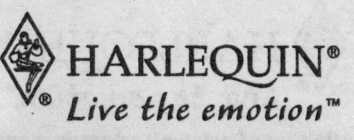